THAÏS

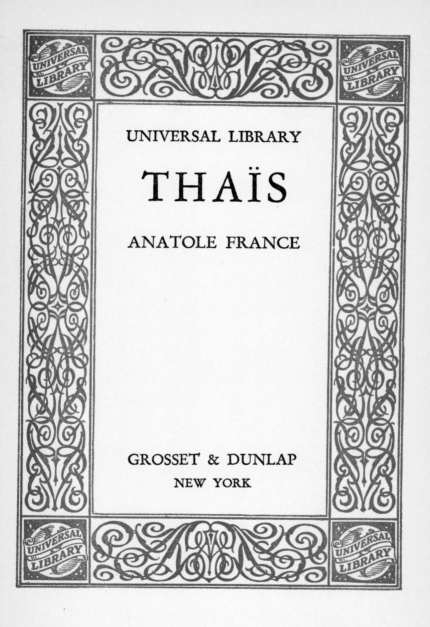

UNIVERSAL LIBRARY

THAÏS

ANATOLE FRANCE

GROSSET & DUNLAP

NEW YORK

CONTENTS

I

THE LOTUS

THE LOTUS

IN THOSE days the desert was peopled with anchorites. Upon each bank of the Nile numerous huts, built of branches and clay by hermits, were scattered at various distances apart, in such a way that those who dwelt in them could live in isolation, and yet assist each other in time of need. Churches, surmounted by a cross, rose up here and there high above the huts, and the monks assembled in them on feast days to assist in celebrating the Mysteries and to participate in the Sacraments. There were, too, right on the banks of the river, houses in which the Cenobites, each of whom was confined to his narrow cell, united solely in order to better preserve their solitude.

The Anchorites and Cenobites lived abstemiously; eating nothing until after sunset and then only taking bread with a little salt and hyssop. Some buried themselves in the sand, making their home in a cavern or tomb, and leading a still more singular existence.

They all wore a hood and robe, slept upon the bare earth after long vigils, prayed, sang psalms, and every day performed masterpieces of penitence. In consideration of original sin, they denied their bodies not only pleasure and gratification, but even that attention which today is considered indispensable. They considered that physical maladies made the soul more healthy, and that the flesh could receive no more glorious adornments than ulcers and sores. Thus were fulfilled the words of the prophets, who said: "The deserts shall be covered with flowers."

Some of the guests of this holy Thebaid spent their time in asceticism and contemplation, while others earned their living by plaiting palm fibers, or hired themselves to neighboring farmers during harvest. The Gentiles falsely suspected some of living by robbery and of joining the wandering Arabs, who pillaged caravans; but in truth these monks despised riches and the scent of their virtues went up to heaven.

Angels, in appearance like young men, came staff in hand as travelers to visit the hermitages, while demons, assuming the shapes of Ethiopians or animals, wandered around the hermits to tempt them. When, in the morning, the monks went to fill their pitchers at the fountain, they saw the footprints of Satyrs in the sand. Considered in its true and spiritual aspect, the Thebaid was a battlefield on which, at all hours and particularly during the night, wonderful combats between heaven and hell were fought.

The ascetics, being furiously assailed by legions of the damned, defended themselves, with the aid of God and the angels, with weapons of fasting, penitence and maceration. Sometimes the spur of carnal desires wounded them so cruelly that they groaned with pain, their moans being similar to the howls of famished hyenas. Then it was that the demons appeared to them in forms of beauty; for though demons are in reality ugly, they sometimes assume an outward beauty in order to veil their inner nature. The ascetics of the Thebaid saw with terror in their cells pictures of pleasure, unknown even to the voluptuous of that century; but, as the sign of the Cross was upon them, they did not succumb to temptation, and the evil spirits, assuming their own shapes, fled away at dawn shameful and raging. It was not uncommon to meet one of them at daybreak fleeing in tears, and, when asked, replying: "I am weeping and groaning because one of the Christians who dwell here has beaten me with rods, and has ignominiously driven me away."

The old men of the desert understood their power over sinners. Their goodness was sometimes terrible. They possessed from the Apostles the power of punishing offences against the true God, and nothing could save those whom they condemned. In the towns, and as far as Alexandria, people whispered in terror that the earth opened to swallow up those sinners who were struck by the rods of these old men. For this reason they were greatly feared by all who lived a vicious life, and particularly by pantomimes, buffoons, married priests and courtesans.

So great was the virtue of these good men that even wild beasts submitted to their authority, and when a hermit was on the point of death a lion came to him to dig his grave with its claws. The holy man, knowing by this event that God would shortly call him hence, embraced all his brethren, and then lay down cheerfully to sleep in the Lord.

Now since Anthony, who was more than a hundred years old, had retired to Mount Colzin with his beloved disciples Macairus and Amathus, there was no monk in all the Thebaid more abounding in good works than Paphnutius, priest of Antinoë. Ephrem and Serapion, to be sure, commanded a larger number of monks, and were renowned for the spiritual and temporal conduct of their monasteries. But Paphnutius observed the most rigorous fasts, and sometimes remained three whole days without nourishment. He wore a robe of rough hair, whipped himself morning and evening, and often prostrated himself upon his face.

His twenty-four disciples, after building their huts near his, imitated his austerities. He loved them dearly in Jesus Christ, and ceaselessly exhorted them to penitence. Among his spiritual sons were men who, after being brigands for many years, were so touched by the exhortations of the holy abbot that they had embraced the monastic life. The purity of their lives elevated their companions. Among them was the cook of the Queen of Abyssinia, who, after being converted by the holy abbot, shed tears without ceasing, and also the deacon Flavian, who was a man of learning and a skilful orator. But the most admirable of the disciples of Paphnutius was a young peasant named Paul, who was called the Simple on account of his extreme innocence. Men laughed at his candor; but God favored him by sending him visions, and by granting him the gift of prophecy.

Paphnutius sanctified his hours by instructing his disciples, and by the practice of asceticism. He, too, often meditated upon the sacred books to discover allegories in them, for which reason though still young he had many virtues. The devils who made such vigorous assaults upon the holy anchorites dared not approach him. At night seven little jackals sat listening before his hut in silence: it was said that they were seven demons whom he retained at his door by virtue of his sanctity.

Paphnutius was born at Alexandria of a noble family, and had been carefully instructed in profane literature. He had even been seduced by the lies of the poets, and, in his early youth, such were the errors of his mind and the disorder of his thoughts, that he believed the human race had been drowned by the deluge of Deucalion, and disputed with his fellow pupils as to the nature, attributes, and even the existence of God. In those days he lived a life of dissipation, this being the fashion among the Gentiles, and now recalled the past with shame for his own confusion. At that time he used to tell his brethren that he boiled in the caldron of false delight, by which he meant that he ate viands skilfully served and frequented public baths. As a matter of fact, up to his twentieth year he had led the life of the century—which should rather be called death than life—but after receiving instruction from the priest Macrinus he became a new man.

The truth took entire possession of him, and he used to say that it had entered into him like a sword. He embraced the faith of Calvary and adored the crucified Christ. After his baptism he remained for another year among the Gentiles, bound by the chains of habit. But upon entering a church one day he heard a deacon read this verse of Scripture: "If thou wilt be perfect, go and sell that thou hast and give to the poor." He at once sold his property, distributed the proceeds in charity, and entered upon a monastic life.

During the ten years which he had spent in solitude, he had not boiled in the caldron of carnal delights, but had anointed himself with profit in the balm of penitence.

One day when, according to his pious custom, he was recalling the hours which he had spent far from God, and was examining his faults one by one in order to exactly understand their enormity, he remembered having seen years before at the theatre of Alexandria an actress of great beauty named Thaïs. This woman took part in the games and was not ashamed to join in skilful dances, the movements of which recalled the most terrible passions. Or else she enacted some of the scenes of shame which the Pagan fables attribute to Venus, Leda, or Pasiphaë. Thus she inflamed all the spectators with the fire of luxury; and when fine young men or rich old men, full of love, came and hung garlands of flowers at her door, she received them kindly. So that, in destroying her own soul, she also destroyed a number of others.

Paphnutius, too, had been one of her admirers. She had aroused the fever of desire in his veins, and on one occasion he had approached her house; but he halted at the door, stayed by the natural timidity of extreme youth (he was only fifteen) and by the fear of being expelled. God in his pity had taken this means of saving him from a great crime. At that time, however, Paphnutius did not recognize this, because he could not then discern between his real interests and his false desires. Then, kneeling in his hut before the image of that saving wood, from which the ransom of the world was suspended as in a balance, Paphnutius began to think of Thaïs, because she was his sin, and he meditated long according to the rules of asceticism upon the fearful horror of carnal delights, the taste for which this woman had inspired in him in the days of trouble and ignorance. After some hours of meditation the image of Thaïs appeared to him with extreme clearness. He saw her again, beautiful in the flesh as she was at the time of his temptation. She appeared first as Leda, lying on a bed of hyacinth, head thrown back, eyes humid and full of light, nostrils quivering, mouth half open, full round breasts, and arms fresh as running streams. At this vision Paphnutius beat his breast, and said: "My God, I call Thee to witness that I perceive the grossness of my sin!"

Her image gradually changed in expression. As the corners of her mouth drooped, the lips of Thaïs slowly revealed mysterious suffering. Her eyes were full of tears and light, from her breast the breath came like the first gusts of the storm. Seeing her thus, Paphnutius was touched to the quick, and throwing himself upon his knees he offered up this prayer:—"O THOU, who hast put pity in our hearts, as the morning dew on the meadows, O Just and Pitiful God, be blessed! Praise be unto Thee! Take away from me this false tenderness which leads to desire, and by thy grace cause me to love thy creatures only in thyself, for they pass away and thou remainest. If I am grieved for this woman, it is because she is thy handiwork. Even the angels bend toward her in solicitude. Is she not, O Lord, the breath of thy mouth? She must not continue sinning with so many citizens and strangers. A great pity for her has arisen in my heart. Her crimes are abominable, and the thought of them alone makes me shudder so that my hair stands up in affright. But the greater her sin the more I must pity her. I weep at the thought that devils will torment her through all eternity."

As he meditated thus he saw a little jackal seated at his feet: this greatly surprised him as the door of his hut had been shut since the morning. The animal seemed to read the priest's thoughts and wagged its tail like a dog. Paphnutius crossed himself; the beast disappeared. Knowing by this that for the first time the devil had entered his hut, he offered up a short prayer. Then he thought again of Thaïs. "With the help of God," he said to himself, "I must save her." Then he slept.

The following morning, after prayer, he visited the holy man Palemon, who led the life of a hermit a short distance away, and found him peaceful and smiling, and digging his garden as was his custom. Palemon was an old man and had a small garden: wild beasts came and licked his hands and the devils did not torment him.

"God be praised! brother Paphnutius," said he, resting on his spade.

"God be praised!" replied Paphnutius. "And peace be with you, brother!"

"Peace be with you also! brother Paphnutius," replied Palemon, as he wiped the sweat from his brow.

"Brother Palemon, the sole object of our conversation should be the praise of the one who has promised to be in the midst of those who assemble in his name. That is the reason I come to talk with you about a plan I have formed to glorify the Lord."

"May the Lord bless thy plan, Paphnutius, as he has blessed my lettuce! Every morning he sheds grace upon my garden with his dew, and his goodness incites me to glorify him in the cucumbers and pumpkins which he gives me. Let us pray him to keep us in his peace, for nothing is more to be feared than the disorderly motions which trouble the heart. When these motions disturb us we are like drunken men, and we walk, wavering to the right or to the left, always ready to fall ignominiously. Sometimes these transports plunge us into intemperate joy, and the man who abandons himself is the cause of the thick laughter of the brutes which echoes through the air. This lamentable joy involves the sinner in all sorts of confusion. But sometimes, too, the troubles of the soul and senses bring an unholy sadness, a thousand times more fatal than joy. Brother Paphnutius, I am only a poor sinner, but during my long life I have discovered that the Cenobite has no worse enemy than sadness. I mean by that the tenacious melancholy which envelops the soul like a fog and conceals the light of God. Nothing is more adverse to safety, and the devil's greatest triumph is to plant a black and bitter disposition in the heart of a good man. If he only sent joyous temptations against us he would not be half so terrible. Alas! he excels in afflicting us. Did he not show our father Anthony a black child so beautiful that it made him weep? With the aid of God, our father Anthony avoided the demon's snares. I have known him the whole of the time he has lived among us; he rejoiced with his disciples and never once became melancholy. But have you not come, brother, to talk of a plan which you have formed? If you will connect me with it, I shall consider it a favor, as its object is the glorification of God."

"Brother Palemon, I indeed propose to glorify the Lord. Fortify me with your counsel, for you are enlightened and sin has never obscured the clearness of your intellect."

"Brother Paphnutius, I am not worthy to untie the strap of your sandal, and my iniquities are as countless as the sands of the desert. But I am old, and will not refuse you the aid of my experience."

"I will confide in you then, brother Palemon, that I am stricken with grief at the thought that there is in Alexandria a courtesan, named Thaïs, who lives in sin and remains an object of scandal to the people."

"Brother Paphnutius, that indeed is a sad abomination. Many women live in this manner among the Gentiles. Have you thought of a remedy applicable to so grave a malady?"

"Brother Palemon, I will go and seek this woman in Alexandria, and with God's help, I will convert her. That is my plan; does it not meet with your approval, brother?"

"Brother Paphnutius, I am nothing but a poor sinner, but

our father Anthony used to say: 'Wheresoever you may be, haste not to leave that place for another.' "

"Do you, brother Palemon, see anything evil in the enterprise which I have conceived?"

"Paphnutius, God keeps me from suspecting my brother's intentions, but our father Anthony also said: 'Fish, which are put upon dry land, die: in the same way, monks who leave their cells and mix with the world deviate from their holy purpose.' "

After saying this, Palemon drove his spade into the earth and began to dig up the soil around a fig tree laden with fruit: while he dug, an antelope which had jumped the garden hedge, stopped surprised and restless, and then in two bounds came up to the old man and slid its fine head into his bosom.

"God be praised in the gazelle of the desert," said Palemon.

He then went into his hut, followed by the graceful animal, and procured some black bread which the antelope ate out of his hand.

Paphnutius remained long in thought with his eyes fixed upon the ground. Then he walked back slowly to his hut, carefully thinking over what he had just heard.

"This hermit," he said to himself, "is a man of great experience; the spirit of prudence is in him. He doubts the wisdom of my plan. However, it would be cruel of me to abandon Thaïs any longer to the demon which possesses her. May God guide and counsel me!"

As he walked along, he saw a plover caught in the net which a hunter had stretched upon the sand, and he knew it was a female bird, for the male bird came flying to the net and broke the meshes one by one with his beak till he had made an opening large enough to allow his mate to escape. The man of God contemplated this scene and as, by virtue of his sanctity, he easily read the mystic meaning of events, he knew that the captive bird was none other than Thaïs, taken in the lakes of abomination, and that, following the example of the plover which had broken the meshes with his beak, he must break with words of power the invisible bonds that bound down Thaïs in sin. He therefore praised God and was confirmed in his resolution. But when he saw the plover entangled by the claws in the net which he had broken, he became uncertain once more.

He did not sleep all night, and before dawn had a vision. Thaïs appeared to him again. Her face did not show any signs of guilty pleasure, nor was she clothed as usual in diaphanous draperies. A shroud enveloped her entirely, and even concealed part of her face, so that the priest could only see two eyes filled with great white tears.

He, too, began to weep, and thinking the vision had come to him from God hesitated no longer. He rose, took a knotty staff (the image of the Christian faith), left his hut, carefully closing the door so that the birds and beasts of the desert could not destroy or injure the book of the Scriptures which he kept at the head of his bed, and called Flavian the deacon to entrust to his care his twenty-three disciples. Then, clad simply in a long cloak, he made his way towards the Nile, intending to follow the Lybian bank to the city founded by the Macedonian. He began to walk over the sand at sunrise, despising fatigue, hunger and thirst, and the sun was almost below the horizon when he saw the dreadful river rolling its blood-stained waters between rocks of gold and fire. He walked along the bank, begging bread at the doors of the huts isolated for the love of God, and cheerfully received abuse, refusals and threats. He feared neither brigands nor wild beasts, but took good care to turn aside from villages and towns along the route. He was afraid to meet children playing at huckle-bones in front of their homes, or to see women in blue robes put down their pitchers on the edge of the water tanks. Everything is dangerous to the hermit; sometimes it is dangerous for him to read in the Scriptures that the Divine Master went from town to town and supped with the disciples. The virtues which the Anchorites carefully embroider upon the tissue of their faith are as fragile as they are magnificent: a breath from the world will tarnish their beautiful doors. For that reason Paphnutius refrained from entering the towns, fearing lest his heart might soften at the sight of men.

He traveled along the bypaths. When evening came, the murmur of the tamarisks, caressed by the breeze, made him tremble and pull down his hood over his eyes to shut out Nature's beauty. After six days' journeying he reached a place called Silsile. There the river flows through a narrow valley bounded on each side by mountains of granite. There the Egyptians, when they adored demons, carved their idols. Paphnutius saw an enormous Sphinx's head still standing among the rocks. Fearing it might be animated by some diabolical power, he made the sign of the Cross and pronounced the name of Jesus; a bat immediately flew out from one of the Sphinx's ears, and Paphnutius knew that he had driven out the evil spirit which had resided there for many centuries. His zeal increased, and seizing a great stone he hurled it at the idol's face. Then the mysterious visage of the Sphinx became so sad that Paphnutius was moved with compassion. In fact, the expression of superhuman grief upon this face of stone would have moved the most callous. Therefore Paphnutius said to the Sphinx:

"O Beast, confess the divinity of Christ Jesus, and I will bless you in the name of the Father, the Son, and the Holy Ghost!"

As he spoke, a red light shone from the eyes of the Sphinx; the beast's heavy eyelids quivered and the lips of granite painfully articulated, like an echo of the human voice, the holy name of Jesus Christ. Then Paphnutius stretched forth his right hand and blessed the Sphinx of Silsile.

He at once resumed his journey, and as the valley opened

out saw the ruins of a mighty city. The temples that were still standing were supported by idols which served as columns, and with God's consent all, from women's heads to animals' horns, fixed upon Paphnutius a steadfast gaze which made him pale. He walked thus seventeen days, eating herbs only, and sleeping at night in the crumbling palaces among the wild cats and rats of the Pharaohs, with which mingled women whose bodies ended in the scales of fish. But Paphnutius knew that these women came from hell, and he drove them away by making the sign of the Cross.

On the eighteenth day, he discovered a miserable palm leaf hut, far away from any village, and buried by the wind in the sand of the desert, and approached it hoping to find it inhabited by some pious Anchorite. As there was no door he could see a pitcher, a heap of onions, and a bed of dry leaves inside.

"That is," he said to himself, "the furniture of an ascetic. Hermits, as a rule, do not wander far from their huts. I shall soon meet this man. I desire to give him the kiss of peace, according to the example of the holy hermit Anthony who, traveling near the abode of the hermit Paul, embraced him three times. We will talk of things eternal, and perhaps our Lord will send us, by a raven, bread which my host will invite me to break in honor."

While he thus spoke to himself, he walked round the hut seeking the hermit. He had not gone a hundred yards when he saw a man sitting cross-legged on the bank of the Nile. The man was naked; his hair and beard were entirely white, and his body was of a deep red color. Paphnutius had no doubt that he was the hermit, and saluted him with the monks' usual greeting.

"Peace be with you, brother! may you one day taste the sweet joys of Paradise!"

The man did not reply, but remained motionless and appeared not to hear. Paphnutius imagined that his silence was caused by one of those transports saints often enjoy. He knelt with clasped hands by the unknown's side and remained thus in prayer till sunset. Then, seeing his companion had not moved, he said to him:

"Father, if you have recovered from the transport in which I have seen you, give me your benediction in our Lord Jesus Christ!"

The other replied, without turning his head: "Stranger, I know not what you mean, nor this Lord Jesus Christ."

"What!" cried Paphnutius. "The prophets have foretold him; legions of martyrs have confessed his name; Cæsar himself has adored him, and but a short time ago I had his glory proclaimed by the Sphinx of Silsile. Is it possible that you know him not?"

"Friend," replied the other, "it is possible. It would even be certain were there any certainty in the world."

Paphnutius was surprised and grieved at this man's incredible ignorance.

"If you know not Jesus Christ," he said to him, "your works will avail you nothing, and you will not gain eternal life."

The old man replied:

"It is vain to act or to refrain; life or death is indifferent to me."

"What!" asked Paphnutius, "you do not desire to live eternally? But, are you not dwelling in this desert in a hut after the manner of the Anchorites?"

"It would appear so."

"Are you not naked and deprived of everything?"

"It would appear so."

"Do you not live on roots and practice chastity?"

"It would appear so."

"Have you not renounced all the vanities of this world?"

"In truth, I have renounced those vain things which are usually men's care."

"So you are as I am, poor, chaste, and a hermit. But you are not as I am in the love of God and in the sight of celestial felicity. Why are you virtuous if you do not believe in Jesus Christ? Why do you deprive yourself of this world's treasure if you do not hope for treasure in heaven?"

"Stranger, I deprive myself of nothing, and I flatter myself that I have found a manner of life satisfying enough, though, to be exact, it is neither a good nor a bad life. Nothing is in itself honorable or shameful, just or unjust, agreeable or painful, good or bad. It is opinion which gives things qualities, as salt savors meats."

"Then in your opinion, there is no certainty. You deny the truth which idolaters themselves have sought. You live in ignorance, like a tired dog sleeping in the mire."

"It is as useless to revile philosophers as to revile dogs. We do not know what a dog is, nor do we knew what we ourselves are. We know nothing."

"Old man, do you then belong to that ridiculous sect called Sceptics? Are you then one of those miserable fools who deny both movement and repose, and know not how to distinguish the light of the sun from the shades of the night?"

"My friend, I am indeed a sceptic, and belong to a sect which, though it seems ridiculous to you, appears good to me. For the same things have diverse appearances. The Pyramids of Memphis are at sunrise cones of rosy light: at sunset they appear like black triangles in a flaming sky. But who will penetrate their inmost substance? You reproach me with denying appearances, when, in fact, appearances are the sole realities which I recognize. The sun appears to me luminous, but its nature is unknown to me. I feel that fire burns, but know not how or why. My friend, you think very ill of me; but thoughts make no difference."

"Why do you live upon dates and onions in the desert? Why do you endure great privations? I endure as great and like you practice abstinence in solitude; but I do it to please

God and to merit eternal beatitude. That is a reasonable aim, for it is wise to suffer with a view to a great reward. On the other hand, it is madness to expose oneself willingly to useless fatigue and vain suffering. If I did not believe—pardon this blasphemy, O uncreated Light!—if I did not believe in the truth of God's teaching by the voices of his prophets, by the example of his Son, by the acts of the apostles, by the authority of councils, and by the witness of martyrs; if I did not know that bodily suffering was necessary for the health of the soul, if I were as you, steeped in ignorance of the sacred mysteries, I should immediately return to the world, should set myself to obtain wealth and to live in luxury, and should say to the children of pleasure: 'Come, my daughters, come, my servants, come all and pour out your wines, philters and perfumes before me.' But you, foolish man, deprive yourself of all comforts; you lose without gaining anything; you give without hope of return, and imitate in ridicule the admirable works of our Anchorites, just as an impudent monkey thinks that by daubing a wall he is copying the picture of a clever painter. O, most stupid of men, what then are your reasons?"

Paphnutius said this with great vehemence. But the old man remained quiet, and said gently:

"Friend, what matter the reasons of a dog sleeping in the mire and a mischievous monkey?"

Paphnutius' sole object was the glory of God. His anger was gone; he accused himself with noble humility.

"Forgive me, my brother," said he, "if zeal for the truth has carried me beyond the proper bounds. God is my witness that it is your error and not your person that I hate. It pains me to see you in darkness, for I love you in Jesus Christ and my heart is filled with care for your salvation. Speak, give me your reasons: I am burning to know them in order that I may refute them."

The old man gently replied:

"I am as much inclined to speech as to silence. I will give you my reason without asking yours in return, for you do not interest me in any way. I have no thought for your happiness or misfortune, and your views are of the utmost indifference to me. How should I love or hate you? Aversion and sympathy are equally unworthy of the sage. But, since you ask me, my name is Timocles, and I was born at Cos, of parents who acquired wealth in business. My father armed ships. His intelligence bore a great resemblance to that of Alexander the Great. He was, however, less dense. In short, his was a man's poor nature. I had two brothers, who became armorers like him. But I turned my attention to the arts. Now my eldest brother was forced by our father to marry a Corian woman named Timaessa, who was so distasteful to him that he could not live with her without becoming melancholy. Timaessa, however, inspired in my youngest brother a criminal love which soon became a furious mania. The Corian hated them both. She loved a flute-player, and received him at night. One morning he left behind the crown he wore at feasts, upon finding which my two brothers swore to kill him, and on the morrow he was killed by the lash, in spite of his tears and prayers. My sister-in-law lost her reason through despair, and these three wretches became like wild beasts, wandering in their madness about Cos, howling like wolves, foaming at the mouth, their eyes fixed upon the ground, amid the shouts of the children who threw shells at them. They died, and my father buried them. Shortly after, his stomach refused all nourishment and he died of hunger, though wealthy enough to buy all the food and fruit in all the marts of Asia. He was grieved at leaving me his fortune. I spent it in travel. I visited Italy, Greece, and Africa without meeting anyone wise or happy. I studied philosophy at Athens and Alexandria, and I was stunned by the violence of the discussions. At last, when I had gone as far as India, I saw upon the banks of the Ganges a naked man who had been there motionless, with his legs crossed, for thirty years. Creepers clung around his emaciated body, while in his hair birds built their nests. But he was alive. Upon seeing him I thought of Timaessa, the flute player, my two brothers, and my father, and I understood that this Indian was wise. 'Men suffer,' I said to myself, 'because they are deprived of what they believe to be a benefit, or else, possessing it, they fear to lose it; or because they suffer that which they believe to be a wrong. Suppress all belief of this kind, and all evils would disappear.' That is the reason why, following the Indian's example, I decided to no longer consider anything advantageous, to profess entire detachment from this world's goods, and to live in solitude and immobility."

Paphnutius had listened to the old man's story with attention.

"Timocles of Cos," he replied, "I confess that everything in your purpose is not without sense. It is wise, for instance, to despise this world's goods; but it would be madness to despise the eternal, and to expose oneself to God's anger in the same way. I deplore your ignorance, Timocles, and I will instruct you in the truth, so that knowing that a God exists in three hypostases you may obey this God as a son obeys his father."

But Timocles interrupted him:

"Restrain yourself, stranger, from expounding your doctrines, and do not attempt to constrain me to share your opinions. All discussion is sterile. My opinion is to have no opinion. I live exempt from troubles, provided that I live without preferences. Resume your way, and do not attempt to draw me from the blessed apathy in which I am plunged, as in a delicious bath, after the rough toil of my life."

Paphnutius was deeply learned in the doctrines of the faith. By his knowledge of the hearts of men he knew that the grace of God was not with the old man Timocles, and that the day of salvation was not yet come to that soul

implacable at its loss. He made no reply, for fear that edification might turn to scandal; for it sometimes happens that disputes with the unfaithful urge them into sin, instead of converting them. For that reason those who possess the truth
should publish it abroad with prudence.

"Farewell, then," said he, "unfortunate Timocles."

Heaving a deep sigh, he resumed his pious journey in the
darkness.

In the morning he saw ibis standing motionless, on one
foot, on the banks of the river, which reflected their pale and
rosy necks. The willows extended their soft grey foliage far
along the bank; cranes flew in triangles in the clear sky, and
among the reeds sounded the cries of invisible herons.

As far as the eye could see, the river rolled its broad green
waves on which, like the wings of birds, sails glided here and
there; white houses stood on the banks at intervals, with light
vapors hovering round them, while from the shade of islands,
weighed down with palms, flowers and fruit, escaped a noisy
multitude of ducks, geese, flamingoes and teal. On the left
the green valley stretched out to meet the desert, its fields and
orchards quivering with joy, the sun gilded the ears, and the
earth's fecundity was exhaled in odorous dust.

Then Paphnutius fell down on his knees and cried:

"Blessed be the Lord who has favored my journey!
Thou God, who spread'st the dawn upon the fig trees of
Arsinoitides, send down thy grace upon the soul of this Thaïs
whom thou hast fashioned with no less love than the flowers
and trees of the field. Make her to flower by thy care as a
balsamic rose in thy celestial Jerusalem!"

Each time he saw a tree in bloom or a brilliant bird he
thought of Thaïs. Thus, along the left bank of the river,
through fertile and populous countries, he in a few days
reached Alexandria, surnamed the beautiful and golden by
the Greeks. It was an hour after daybreak when he saw the
mighty city from the summit of a hill, its roofs sparkling in

the rosy morn. He stopped, and folding his arms upon his breast, said:

"There then is the delightful spot where I was born in sin, the air from which I breathed poisoned perfumes, the sea of pleasure upon which I heard the Sirens sing! There is my cradle according to the flesh, there my home according to the world! A cradle of flowers and a home of nobility in the eyes of men! It is natural, Alexandria, for children to cherish you as a mother, and I was reared upon your breasts decked in magnificence. But the ascetic despises nature, the mystic disdains appearances, the Christian regards his human home as a place of exile, and the monk shuns the world. I have turned away my heart from love for you, Alexandria. I hate you! I hate you for your wealth, for your science, for your gentleness and for your beauty. My curse be upon you, temple of demons! Gentile couch of shame, tainted Aryan see, my curse be upon you! O Son of God, who led the holy hermit Anthony our father when, coming from the depths of the desert, he entered this citadel of idolatry to confirm the faith of the confessors and the courage of the martyrs; angel of beauty, invisible child, God's earliest breath, fly before me and with the beating of your wings perfume the corrupted air I am about to breathe among the princes of darkness of this world!"

After praying thus, he resumed his journey. He entered the city by the gate of the Sun. This gate was of stone, and stood up proudly. But reclining in its shade wretches offered for sale to the passers-by citrons and figs, or with their lamentations begged an obol.

A ragged old woman who was kneeling there seized the monk's robe and kissing it said:

"Man of God, bless me so that God may also bless me. I have suffered many things in this world, and I desire joy in the next. You come from God, holy man, and so the dust of your feet is more precious than fine gold."

"God be praised," said Paphnutius, as with half open hand he placed the sign of redemption upon the old woman's head.

But hardly had he gone twenty paces along the street when a crowd of children began to throw stones at him, crying:

"Oh, wicked monk! He is blacker than a raven, and more bearded than a goat. He is a drone. Why not hang him in a field, like a Priapus, to frighten the birds? No, he would bring down hail upon the apple blossoms. He brings bad luck. To the ravens with him!" Stones accompanied these last words.

"God bless these poor children," murmured Paphnutius.

As he pursued his way, he thought:

"I am venerated by the old woman and despised by the children. Thus the same object is differently appreciated by men, who are uncertain in their judgment and are subject to error. It must be admitted that for a Gentile, the old man Timocles is not void of sense. In his blindness he perceives that he is deprived of light. Everything in this world is mirage and shifting sand. Stability is in God alone."

He traversed the city with a rapid step. After ten years' absence he recognized each stone, and each stone was to him a stone of scandal, recalling a sin. Therefore he roughly trampled with his naked feet the stones of the street, and rejoiced as he saw upon them the blood of his mangled heels. Leaving on the left the magnificent porticoes of the temple of Serapis, he walked along a road bordered by magnificent villas, which seemed steeped in perfume. Pines, maples, and turpentine trees lifted their heads above red cornice and golden acroteria. Through the half-open doors he saw statues of brass in marble vestibules and streams of water among the foliage; no sounds disturbed the peace of these lovely retreats, nothing but the distant sound of a flute. The monk stopped before a small but nobly proportioned house, supported by columns as graceful as young girls. It was ornamented with bronze busts of the most famous Greek philosophers.

Among them he saw Plato, Socrates, Aristotle, Epicurus and Zeno, and after knocking he thought, as he waited: "It is vain for metal to glorify these false sages. Their untruths are confounded; their souls are plunged in hell, and Plato, the famous, who filled the land with the power of his eloquence, is now disputing with devils."

A slave opened the door, and finding a man with naked feet upon the mosaic of the porch, said roughly:

"Go and beg elsewhere, ridiculous monk, and do not wait for me to drive you away with a stick."

"Brother," replied the priest of Antinöe, "I simply desire you to take me to Nicias, your master."

The slave replied still more angrily:

"My master does not receive dogs like you."

"Son," replied Paphnutius, "please do as I ask, and tell your master I desire to see him."

"Off you go," shouted the furious porter.

He raised his staff to the holy man, who, crossing his arms upon his breast, received, without moving, the blow full on his face, and then gently repeated:

"Do as I desire, my son, I beg you."

Then the trembling porter murmured:

"Who is this man who does not fear to suffer?"

He ran to tell his master.

Nicias was having his bath. He was a gracious smiling man. He wore an expression of gentle irony upon his face. As he saw the monk approach, he rose and advanced with open arms:

"What, you, Paphnutius," he cried, "my fellow disciple, friend and brother! I can still recognize you, though you have become more like a wild beast than a man. Embrace me. Do you recollect the time we studied grammar, rhetoric and philosophy together? Even then you had a somber and savage humor, but I loved you because of your perfect sincerity. We used to say that you saw the universe through a horse's wild eyes, and it was not surprising that you were distrustful. You were a little lacking in atticism, but your liberality knew no bounds. You set no store either by your money or your life. There was, too, in you a strange genius, a strange spirit, which interested me greatly. I am, indeed, glad to see you after ten years' absence. You have left the desert; you are giving up Christian superstition and resuming your old life. This is indeed a red-letter day.

"Crobyle and Myrtale," he added, turning to his slaves, "perfume my dear guest's feet, hands and beard."

They brought the ewer and phials and metal mirror with a smile. But Paphnutius with an imperious gesture stayed them, and cast down his eyes, so that he might not see them, for they were naked. Nicias, however, gave him cushions and offered him food and drink of various kinds, all of which he contemptuously declined.

"Nicias," said he, "I have not given up what you wrongly call the Christian superstition, and what is indeed the truth of truths. In the beginning was the Word, and the Word was with God, and the Word was God. Everything was made by him, and without him was nothing made that was made. In him was life, and the life was the light of men."

"Dear Paphnutius," replied Nicias, as he put on a perfumed tunic, "do you think you will astonish me by quoting unskilfully arranged words, which are only a vain murmur? Have you forgotten that I myself am something of a philosopher? Do you think you can content me with a few shreds torn from the purple of Amelius, when Amelius, Porphyrius and Plato, in all their glory, fail to satisfy me? Systems constructed by sages are only stories imagined to amuse men's eternal infancy. We must smile at them, as we do at the stories of the ass, the Matron of Ephesus, or any other Milesian fable." Taking his guest by the arm, he led him into a hall, in which were thousands of rolls of papyrus in baskets. "Here is my library," he said; "it contains a small number of the systems which philosophers have constructed to explain the world. The Serapeum with all its wealth does not contain them all. Alas, they are only sick men's dreams."

He forced his guest to sit in an ivory chair, and sat down himself. Paphnutius threw a sorrowful glance at the books in the library, and said:

"They must all be burnt."

"O, my guest, what a loss that would be!" replied Nicias; "for sometimes sick men's dreams are amusing. Besides, if all the dreams and visions of men were to be destroyed, the earth would lose its forms and colors, and we should all sleep in sorrowful stupidity."

Paphnutius continued his idea:

"It is certain that the doctrines of the Pagans are only empty dreams. But God, who is the truth, has revealed himself to men by miracles. He was made flesh, and dwelt among us."

Nicias replied:

"You speak well, dear Paphnutius, when you say that he was made flesh. A God who thinks, acts, speaks and walks in nature as ancient Ulysses did, is quite a man. How do you expect belief in this new Jupiter, when the fools in Athens, in the days of Pericles, did not any longer believe in the old Jupiter? But let us leave all that. You have not come, I think, to dispute upon the three hypostases. What can I do for you, fellow disciple?"

"Something exceedingly good," replied the priest of Antinoë. "Lend me a perfumed tunic like the one you have just put on. Add to that golden sandals and a phial of oil to anoint my beard and hair. I shall be glad, too, if you will give me a purse of a thousand drachmæ. That, Nicias, is what I came to ask of you, for the love of God and in memory of our former friendship."

Nicias made Crobyle and Myrtale bring his richest tunic; it was embroidered in the Asiatic style with flowers and ani-

mals. The two women held it open and made its vivid colors
flash, expecting Paphnutius to take off the cloak which covered him from head to foot. But as the monk declared he
would sooner lose his flesh than take off his robe, they passed
the tunic underneath. As these two women were beautiful
they did not fear men, although they were slaves. They
began to laugh at the appearance of this strangely arrayed
monk. Crobyle called him her dear satrap, as she held up the
mirror before him, and Myrtale pulled his beard. But Paphnutius was praying to God, and did not see them. After
putting on the golden sandals and fastening the purse to his
belt, he said to Nicias, who was looking at him with a smile:

"Nicias, the things you see need not be a scandal to your
eyes. Be sure that I will make good use of this tunic, this
purse and these sandals."

"Dear friend," replied Nicias, "I am thinking no evil, for
I believe men equally incapable of good and ill. Good and
evil exist only in opinion. The sage has, for reasons of action,
only custom and habit. I conform to the reigning prejudices
at Alexandria. That is the reason I pass for an honorable
man. Go, friend, and be glad."

But Paphnutius considered that he ought to warn his host
of his plan.

"You know," he said, "the Thaïs who acts at the theater?"

"She is beautiful," replied Nicias, "and there was a time
when she was dear to me. I have sold a mill and two fields
of corn for her, and have composed in her honor three books
of detestable elegies. Surely beauty is the most powerful
thing in the world, and if we were made to possess it forever,
we should think as little as possible of the Divine Word, eons
and all the other reveries of philosophers. But I wonder,
Paphnutius, at your coming from the depths of the Thebaid
to talk of Thaïs."

After saying this, he sighed gently. Paphnutius looked at
him in horror, being unable to conceive how a man could so

quietly avow such a sin. He expected to see the earth open and swallow Nicias up in flames. But the earth remained firm, and the Alexandrian, with his face in his hand, smiled in silence sadly at the images of his departed youth. The monk, rising, replied in a solemn voice:

"Nicias! my object, by God's aid, is to snatch away this Thaïs from base earthly love and give her as a spouse to Jesus Christ. If the Holy Spirit does not forsake me, Thaïs will to-day quit this city to enter a nunnery."

"Fear to offend Venus," replied Nicias, "she is a powerful goddess. She will be angry with you if you take away her most illustrious servant."

"God will protect me," said Paphnutius. "May he send light into your heart, Nicias, and draw you from the abyss in which you are plunged!"

He went out. But Nicias followed him. Rejoining him near the door, he placed his hand upon his shoulder and whispered in his ear:

"Fear to offend Venus; her vengeance is terrible."

Paphnutius, disdaining this warning, went out without turning his head. His conversation with Nicias had strongly inspired him with contempt; but the idea that his friend of the past had received the caresses of Thaïs was quite unbearable. Sin with this woman seemed to him more detestable than any other sin. It aroused in him a singular feeling of malice, and henceforth he execrated Nicias. He had always hated impurity, but surely the image of this vice had never appeared so abominable before; never had he partaken so heartily of Jesus Christ's anger and the angels' sorrow.

He felt a stronger desire to snatch Thaïs from the midst of the Gentiles and longed to see and save the actress. It was always necessary to wait when visiting this woman till the heat of the day was past. The morning was hardly over as Paphnutius walked along the chief streets of the city, and he had resolved to take no nourishment upon the journey so that he might be more worthy of the favor for which he had prayed the Lord. In the supreme bitterness of his soul, he did not dare to enter any of the churches of the city, because he knew they had been profaned by the Aryans, who had overthrown the Lord's tables. In fact these heretics, who were maintained by the Emperor of the East, had driven out the patriarch Athanasius from his episcopal see, and had filled the Christians of Alexandria with fear and dread.

He walked at hazard, sometimes fixing his eyes upon the earth in humility, and at others raising them in ecstasy. After wandering about for some time he found himself upon one of the quays. The harbor sheltered innumerable dark hulled ships, while the treacherous sea smiled in azure and silver in the offing. A galley having a Nereid at the prow was weighing anchor. The oarsmen sang as they rowed; and soon the white daughter of the ocean, covered with humid pearls, became to the monk but a fleeting profile; she sailed with a pilot's aid through the narrow passage into the basin of Eunostos and gained the open sea, leaving behind her a trail of foam.

"I, too," thought Paphnutius, "once desired to embark upon the ocean of the world with a song upon my lips. But I soon recognized my folly, and the Nereid has not overpowered me."

With this in his thoughts he sat down upon a coil of rope and fell asleep. While he slept he saw a vision. He seemed to hear the piercing blast of a trumpet and, as the sky became the color of blood, he knew that the end was come. As he prayed to God with his whole heart, he saw an enormous beast coming to him, having upon its forehead a cross of light, and recognized the Sphinx of Silsile. The beast seized him with its teeth without doing him any injury and carried him off, as a cat does her kittens, dangling from its mouth. Paphnutius in this manner traversed several kingdoms, crossing rivers and mountains, till he came to a scene of desolation

covered with frightful rocks and hot ashes. The earth emitted
from many openings a breath of fire. The beast, gently placing Paphnutius upon the earth, said to him:

"Look!"

Paphnutius leaned over the edge of the abyss and saw a
river of fire flaming through the center of the earth in a
channel of black rocks. There in a fierce light demons tor-
mented the souls of the dead. These souls retained the shapes
of the bodies which had contained them, and even shreds of
clothing remained attached to them. They seemed at peace
in the midst of torment. The soul of a man tall and white,
with a band across his forehead and scepter in his hand, sang
with closed eyes; his voice filled the sterile plain with harmony; he sang of gods and heroes. Little green devils were
piercing his lips and throat with red hot irons. The shade of
Homer continued to sing. Close by old Anaxagoras, bald
and gnarled, traced figures in the dust with his compass. A
demon was pouring boiling oil into the sage's ear without
interrupting his meditations. The monk saw, too, a crowd of
persons upon the dreary bank of the river of fire, reading or
conversing as they walked, like masters and pupils of the
Academy in the shade of the plane trees. Apart, old Timocles
shook his head in denial. An angel of the abyss was waving a
torch under his eyes, and Timocles would see neither.

Dumb with surprise at this sight, Paphnutius turned
towards the beast. It had disappeared, and in its place stood
a veiled woman who said to him:

"Look well and understand. Such is the stubbornness of
these infidels that they remain in hell the victims of illusions
which seduced them on earth. Death has not disabused their
minds, for it is very clear that to see God it is not sufficient to
die. Those you see there, who ignored the truth as men, will
always ignore it. Who are the demons, who rage around these
souls, but forms of divine Justice. For that reason these souls
neither see nor understand. Strangers to truth of all kinds,

they know not their own condemnation, and even God cannot constrain them to suffer."

"God is omnipotent," said the priest of Antinöe.

"He cannot perform an absurdity," replied the veiled woman. "To punish them, it would be necessary to enlighten them, and if they possessed the truth they would be as the elect."

Again Paphnutius, full of horror and uneasiness, leaned over the abyss. This time he saw, under the charred myrtles, the smiling shade of Nicias, his forehead wreathed with flowers. Near him Aspasia of Miletus, attired in her elegant mantle, seemed to speak at once of philosophy and love, so sweet and noble was the expression of her face. The rain of fire which was falling was like the freshness of the dawn to them, and their feet trod the burned-up earth as if it were lovely turf. At this, Paphnutius became furious.

"Strike, my God, strike! It is Nicias," he cried. "Make him weep! make him groan! make him grind his teeth! He has sinned with Thaïs!"

Paphnutius awoke in the arms of a sailor strong as Hercules, who was crying out, as he dragged him on the sand:

"Peace, friend, peace. By Proteus, god of the sea, you sleep restlessly. If I had not held you back, you would have fallen into the Eunostos. As true as my mother sold salt fish, I saved your life."

"Thank God," Paphnutius replied.

Rising to his feet he walked straight before him, meditating upon the vision which had come to him in his sleep.

"This vision," he said to himself, "is manifestly evil; it offends divine goodness by representing hell as devoid of reality. It certainly comes from the Devil."

He reasoned thus because he knew how to discern dreams sent by God from those produced by wicked angels. Such discrimination is useful to the hermit, who lives surrounded by apparitions, for in shunning men he is sure to meet spirits.

The deserts are peopled with phantoms. When pilgrims approached the ruined castle to which the holy Anthony had retired, they heard noises like those of towns *en fête*. These noises were made by the devils tempting the holy man.

Paphnutius recalled this memorable example. He recalled the case of St. John of Egypt, whom for sixty years the Devil tried to seduce by means of spells. But John baffled the ruses of hell. One day, however, the demon, in man's shape, entered the venerable man's grotto and said to him: "John, you must prolong your fast till to-morrow evening." John believing he was listening to an angel's voice, obeyed and fasted on the morrow till the hour of vespers. That was the only victory the Prince of Darkness ever won over St. John the Egyptian, and it was but a paltry one. For that reason it is not at all wonderful that Paphnutius at once recognized the falsity of the vision which had visited him during his sleep.

While he was gently reproaching God for abandoning him to the demon's power, he was pushed and carried along by a crowd of people all hurrying the same way. Being unaccustomed to walking in cities, he was driven from one passer-by to another like an inert mass; and becoming entangled in the folds of his own tunic he almost fell on several occasions. Desirous to know where all these people were going, he asked one of them the reason of his haste.

"Stranger, do you not know," the latter replied, "that the games are about to commence and that Thaïs is appearing? All these citizens are going to the theater, and I am going there too. Would you care to accompany me?"

Suddenly perceiving that it would suit his plan to see Thaïs in the games, Paphnutius followed the stranger. The theater was just in front of them; its portico was adorned with brilliant masks, and its vast circular wall peopled with innumerable statues. Following the crowd, they entered a narrow corridor at the end of which stretched the amphitheater dazzling with light. They took their seats in one of the rows, while the magnificently decorated arena was still empty. No curtain obstructed the view, and the audience could see a mound like those which the ancient nations dedicated to the shades of their heroes. This mound stood in the midst of a camp. Piles of lances stood before tents, and golden shields hung from the tent poles among wreaths of laurel and crowns of oak leaves. The silence of sleep was over all. But a buzzing, like the sound of a hive of bees, arose from the semicircle of spectators. Every face, red with the reflection of purple robes, turned with an expression of expectant curiosity towards the large silent space containing the tomb and tents. The women laughed as they ate citrons.

Paphnutius prayed inwardly and refrained from vain conversation, but his neighbor commenced to complain of the decline of the theater.

"Formerly," said he, "skilled actors declaimed beneath the mask the verses of Euripides and Menander. Now dramas are not spoken, they are only acted, and of the divine spectacles held in honor of Bacchus in Athens, there remains only pose and gesture which a Barbarian or even a Scythian could understand. The tragic mask, in which the voices of the actors were augmented by the clash of metal, the buskin, which made men like gods in stature, the tragic majesty and sweet-versed songs, all have gone. Pantomimes and dancers with uncovered faces replace Paulus and Roscius. What would the Athenians in the days of Pericles have said, had they seen a woman show herself thus at the games? It is indecent for a woman to appear in public. We have indeed degenerated to allow it. As true as my name is Dorion, woman is the enemy of man and the shame of the earth."

"You speak wisely," replied Paphnutius, "woman is our worst enemy. She gives pleasure in that she is to be feared."

"By the eternal gods," cried Dorion, "woman brings man not pleasure, but sorrow, trouble and black care! Love is the cause of our most poignant sorrows. Listen, stranger: in my youth I went to Trezena in Argolis, and I saw a myrtle of wonderful size, the leaves of which were covered with innumerable pin holes. Now this is what the people of Trezena say about the myrtle: 'Queen Phaedra, at the time she began to love Hippolytus, remained all day languishing under this very tree. In her dreadful weariness, she drew the golden pin, which held her blonde hair, and with it pierced the leaves of the shrub. Thus all the leaves were covered with pricks. After destroying the innocent man whom she pursued with her incestuous love, Phaedra, as you know, died in misery. She shut herself in her nuptial chamber and hung herself by her golden girdle from an ivory peg. The gods willed that the myrtle, a witness of this terrible misery, should forever bear upon its leaves the pin pricks.' I plucked one of its leaves; I placed it at the head of my bed, as an ever-present warning to myself not to abandon myself to the furies of love, and to strengthen myself in the doctrine of the divine Epicurus, my master, who teaches that desire is a thing greatly to be feared. Properly speaking, however, love is a malady of faith, and one can never be sure of perfect health."

Paphnutius asked:

"Dorion, what are your pleasures?"

Dorion, in sorrow, replied:

"I have only one pleasure, and that I admit is not a very vivid one; it is meditation. With a weak stomach a man must not seek others."

Taking advantage of these last words, Paphnutius was beginning to initiate the Epicurean in the spiritual joys procured by the contemplation of God. He began:

"Listen to the truth and receive the light!"

As he shouted out this, he saw on all sides of him heads and arms turned towards him, bidding him be silent. A deep silence fell over the theater, through which soon burst the heroic music.

The games commenced. Soldiers had left the tents and begun to prepare for departure, when, by an awful prodigy, a cloud covered the summit of the funeral mound. Then the cloud dispersed, and the shade of Achilles appeared clad in golden armor. Stretching out his arm towards the warriors, he seemed to say: "What! you are departing, children of Greece; you are returning to the land I shall never again see, and you leave my tomb without offerings?" At once the leaders of the Greeks crowded round the base of the mound.

Acamas, son of Theseus, old Nestor, and Agamemnon, bearing the scepter and bands, gazed at the prodigy. Pyrrhus, the young son of Achilles, was prostrate in the dust. Ulysses, recognizable by the cap from which his curly hair escaped, showed by his gestures that he agreed with the hero's shade. He argued with Agamemnon, and from their gestures the audience could understand their words.

"Achilles," the King of Ithaca seemed to say, "is worthy of honor among us, the man who died gloriously for Greece. He asks that the daughter of Priam, the virgin Polyxena, be sacrificed upon his tomb. Greeks, content the hero's manes, and let the son of Peleus rejoice in Hades."

But the King of Kings replied:

"Let us spare the Trojan virgins, whom we have snatched from the altars. Evils enough have fallen upon Priam's illustrious race."

He spoke thus because he loved Polyxena's sister; but sage Ulysses reproached him with preferring Cassandra's couch to the lance of Achilles.

All the Greeks applauded Ulysses with clashing arms. Polyxena's death was decided, and, thus appeased, the shade of Achilles vanished. The music, sometimes furious and sometimes plaintive, followed the thoughts of the characters. The audience burst into applause.

Paphnutius, who ascribed everything to the divine truth, murmured:

"We see by this fable how cruel were the worshipers of false gods."

"All religions were born in crime," replied the Epicurean. "Happily a Greek full of divine wisdom came to free men from the vain terrors of the unknown."

But Hecuba, with disheveled hair and torn robe, came out of the tent where she was a captive. There was a deep sigh when her perfect image of misfortune appeared. Hecuba, warned by a prophetic dream, moaned for herself and her daughter. Ulysses was already at her side asking for Polyxena. The old mother tore out her hair, rent her cheeks with her nails, and kissed the hands of this cruel man, who maintained his pitiless gentleness, and seemed to say:

"Be wise, Hecuba, and yield to necessity. There are old mothers also in our homes, weeping for their children, who forever sleep beneath the pines of Ida."

Cassandra, once the queen of prosperous Asia, now a slave, put dust upon her head.

But at this point the lifting of the tent cloth displayed the virgin Polyxena. An unanimous murmur arose from the spectators. They had recognized Thaïs. Paphnutius saw once more the woman he sought. With her white arm she held above her head the heavy tent cloth. Motionless as a beautiful statue, but throwing from her violet eyes sweet and proud glances all around, she made everyone feel the magic tremor of her beauty.

A murmur of approval arose from the audience, and Paphnutius, clasping his hands upon his heart in agitation, breathed with a sigh:

"Why, O God, dost thou give this power to one of thy creatures?"

Dorion, less moved, said:

"Truly the atoms which compose this woman present an agreeable combination to the eye. It is but one of Nature's frolics, for these atoms know not what they compose. One day they will separate with the same indifference with which they united. Where now are the atoms which composed Laïs or Cleopatra? I do not deny that women are sometimes beautiful. They are, however, made to submit to annoying disgrace and disgusting inconvenience. These things occupy the minds of the thoughtful, while the vulgar pay them no attention. Women inspire love, although it is unreasonable to love them."

Thus the philosopher and the ascetic contemplated Thaïs, and followed each his train of thought. Neither had seen Hecuba turn towards her daughter, and say to her in gesture:

"Try to move cruel Ulysses. Make your tears, your youth, your beauty, speak to him!"

Thaïs, or rather Polyxena herself, let fall the tent door. She moved a step and all hearts were won. When, with a noble, gliding gait, she advanced towards Ulysses, the rhythm of her movements, accompanied by the music of flutes, seemed to render her the divine center of the harmony of the world. The audience saw nothing but her, all the rest being eclipsed by her glory. The action of the scene, however, continued.

The prudent son of Laertes turned his head, and concealed his hand beneath his cloak to avoid the glances and kisses of the suppliant. The virgin signed to him to fear her no more. Her calm glance said:

"Ulysses, I will follow you and obey necessity, because I desire to die. Daughter of Priam and sister of Hector, my couch, formerly judged worthy of kings, shall not receive a foreign master. I freely renounce the light of day."

Hecuba, inert in the dust, suddenly arose and clasped her daughter in a desperate embrace. Polyxena, with resolute gentleness, removed her mother's arms from about her; she appeared to say:

"Mother, do not expose yourself to the outrages of the master. Do not think that he will not drag you roughly from me. Beloved mother, give me your withered hand, and approach your lips to mine."

The beauty of grief was on the face of Thaïs. The crowd recognized this woman's power of thus clothing, with super-human grace, the forms and acts of life; and Paphnutius, pardoning her present splendor for the sake of her approaching humility, gloried in the saint he was about to add to Heaven.

The spectacle reached its climax. Hecuba fell as dead, and Polyxena, led by Ulysses, advanced towards the tomb surrounded by the noblest of the warriors. She climbed, to an accompaniment of mourning chants, the mound, on the summit of which the son of Achilles offered libations in a golden cup to the manes of the hero. When the sacrificers stretched out their arms to seize her, she signed to them her wish to die at liberty, as the descendant of so many kings ought. Then tearing her tunic, she bared her heart. There Pyrrhus with averted head plunged his sword, and by a skilful device, blood flowed in streams from the virgin's dazzling breast, while she, with averted head and the horror of death in her eyes, fell prone.

While the warriors violated the victim, and covered her with lilies and anemones, cries of fright and sobs rent the air, and Paphnutius, rising from his seat, prophesied in a voice of thunder:

"Gentiles, vile worshipers of demons! And Aryans, more infamous than idolaters, learn: What you have just seen is an image and symbol. This fable has a mystic meaning, and soon that woman will be sacrificed, a willing victim, to the resurrected God."

The crowd was already leaving the theater in great numbers. The priest of Antinöe, escaping from the surprised Dorion, gained the exit still prophesying.

An hour later he knocked at Thaïs' door.

The actress dwelt in the wealthy quarter of Racotes near Alexander's tomb, in a house surrounded by shady gardens, containing artificial rockeries, and a stream fringed with poplars. An old black slave, loaded with rings, opened the door and asked his business.

"I desire to see Thaïs," he replied. "God is my witness that I have come only to see her."

As he wore a rich tunic, and spoke with an air of authority, the slave permitted him to enter.

"You will find Thaïs," she said, "in the Nymph's grotto."

II

THE PAPYRUS

THE PAPYRUS

THAÏS was the child of poor though free parents who were idolaters. From her youngest days her father kept an inn much frequented by sailors at Alexandria near the gate of the Moon. A few vivid detached souvenirs of her infancy remained in her mind. She could recall her father as he sat with his legs crossed in the angle of the hearth, a big quiet man, but one to be feared, like one of those old Pharaohs whose memory the chants of complaint uttered by the blind at the crossways preserve. She could recall, too, her thin and sorrowful mother, wandering about the house like a famished cat, and filling it with the sounds of her piercing voice, and the light of her phosphorescent eyes. It was said that she was a magician, and changed into an owl at night to meet her lovers. Rumor lied: Thaïs knew well from frequent observation that her mother had no dealings with the magic arts, but as she was devoured with avarice, she spent the night counting the day's profit. Her inert father and avaricious mother allowed her to shape her life like the animals in the yard. Thus she became very skilful in abstracting obols one by one from the girdles of drunken sailors, and amusing them by naïve songs, and infamous words of whose meaning she was ignorant. She passed from knee to knee in the tavern impregnated with the smell of fermented drinks and resinous bottles; then, with her face sticky with beer, and covered with scratches from the sailor's rough beards, she escaped clasping the obols in her little hands, and ran to buy honeycomb from an old woman in the gate of the Moon. Every day the scenes were the same: the sailors recounted their dangers in times of storm, then played dice or huckle-bones, and called with oaths for the best Cilician beer.

Each night she was awakened by the scuffles of the drinkers. Oyster shells hurled across the tables in the midst of furious uproar wounded their faces. Sometimes by the light of smoky lamps she saw knives gleam and blood flow.

In her early years, the only form of human goodness known to her was in the person of Ahmes, in whom she was humiliated. Ahmes, the slave of the house, was a Nubian blacker than the pots he gravely scoured and as good as a night of sleep. He often took Thaïs upon his knees and told her stories in which there were caverns full of treasure, built for avaricious kings, who put to death the masons and architects. There were too, in these stories, clever thieves, who married Kings' daughters, and courtesans who built pyramids. Little Thaïs loved Ahmes as a father, as a mother, as a nurse, and as a dog. She clung to the slave and followed him to the cellar among the wine jars, and to the yard among the poor ragged hens who fluttered, quicker than eaglets, before the negro's knife. Often at night upon the straw he made water mills and ships large as a hand with all their equipment for Thaïs, instead of sleeping.

From his master's continual ill treatment he had an ear torn off, and his body was covered with scars. His face, however, still wore a peaceful and joyful expression. No one about him thought of asking him whence he drew his soul's consolation and his heart's pacification. He was as simple as a child. When doing his daily work he chanted in a harsh voice canticles which made the child tremble and dream.

Ahmes was a Christian. He had been baptised, and was called Theodore at the feasts of the faithful, which he attended secretly during the time allowed him for sleep.

At this time the Church was undergoing its supreme trial. By the orders of the Emperor, the churches were destroyed, holy books burnt, and holy vessels and candlesticks melted down. Despoiled of their honors, the Christians expected nothing short of death. Terror reigned in the community of Alexandria; the prisons were filled to overflowing with victims. It was whispered in affright among the faithful, that in Syria, Arabia, Mesopotamia, Cappadocia, and the whole empire, whips, wooden horses, iron claws, and wild beasts were rending priests and virgins asunder. Then, Anthony, who was already celebrated for his visions and solitude, the head prophet of the faithful in Egypt, swooped down like an eagle from the top of his rock upon the city of Alexandria, and, passing from church to church, inflamed with his own zeal the entire community. Invisible to the Pagans, he was nevertheless present in all Christian assemblies, inspiring in each the spirit of strength and prudence which animated him. The persecution was particularly severe upon slaves. Many of them in fear denied the faith. Others, in greater numbers, fled to the desert, hoping to live there either in contemplation or by pillage. But Ahmes frequented the assemblies as usual, visited prisoners, buried martyrs, and professed the religion of Christ with joy. Struck by this true zeal, the great Anthony, before returning to the desert, clasped the black slave in his arms, and gave him the kiss of peace.

When Thaïs was seven years old, Ahmes began to speak to her of God.

"The Lord God," he told her, "lived in heaven, like a Pharaoh in the tents of his harem and beneath the trees of his gardens. He was the oldest of the old, more ancient than the world, and had only one son, Prince Jesus, whom he loved with all his heart, and who excelled both virgins and angels in beauty. And the good God said to Prince Jesus:

" 'Leave my harem and palace, my date trees and my fountains. Descend to earth for the good of men. There you will be like a little child and live in poverty among the poor. Suffering will be your daily bread, and so abundant will be your tears, that they will form rivers, in which weary slaves will bathe in delight. Go, my son!'

"Prince Jesus obeyed the Lord, and came to earth at a place called Bethlehem in Judæa. He walked in meadows carpeted with anemones, saying to his companions:

" 'Happy are those who are hungry, for they shall sit at meat with my father! Happy are those who are thirsty, for they shall drink at the fountains of heaven! Happy are those who weep, for I will dry their eyes with veils finer than those of the almées.'

"For that reason the poor loved and believed in him. But the rich hated him, fearing he would set the poor over them. In those days Cleopatra and Cæsar were all powerful on the earth. They both hated Jesus, and ordered the judges and priests to kill him. To obey the Queen of Egypt, the Princes of Syria raised a cross upon a high mountain and upon the cross killed Jesus. But women washed the body and buried it, and Prince Jesus, after breaking the covering of his tomb, ascended to God his father.

"Since that time all those who die in him go to heaven. The Lord God, with open arms, says to them: 'Welcome, since you love the Prince my son. Bathe and eat.'

"They shall bathe to the sounds of beautiful music and all the time they feast they shall see almées dancing and listen to stories without end. The Lord God will hold them dearer to himself than the light of his eyes, as they are his guests, and they shall have pomegranates from his garden."

Ahmes often spoke thus, and so Thaïs learned the truth. She admired it, and said:

"I should like to eat the pomegranates."

Ahmes answered her:

"Only those who are baptised in Jesus will taste the fruits of heaven."

Thaïs asked to be baptised. Seeing by this that she had hope in Jesus, the slave resolved to instruct her more deeply, so that when baptised she might enter the Church. She attached herself closely to him as his daughter in the Spirit.

The child, repulsed by her unjust parents, had no bed under the parental roof. She slept in a corner of the stable among the animals. There each night Ahmes secretly joined her.

He gently approached the straw upon which she slept, and then sat down on his heels with his legs doubled up in the hereditary attitude of his race. His black body and face were lost in the darkness; his great white eyes shone, and from them came a light like a ray of dawn through the chinks of a door. He spoke in a sad chanting voice, having the sorrowful sweetness of music heard in the evening in the streets. Sometimes the bray of a donkey or the soft lowing of an ox accompanied, like a choir of obscured spirits, the voice of the slave as he repeated the Gospel. Out of the darkness came his voice impregnated with zeal, grace and hope; and the neophyte, her hand clasped in the hand of Ahmes, soothed by these monotonous sounds and the vague images of her imagination, slept, calm and smiling, among the harmonies of the dark night and the mysterious saints, in the beams of a star which peeped through the cracks of the stable.

Her initiation lasted an entire year, till the season in which the Christians joyfully keep the Feast of the Passover. One night of that glorious week, Thaïs, who was already asleep upon the straw, felt herself lifted up by the slave, whose eyes gleamed with a new light. He was not, as usual, in rags, but wore a long white cloak, beneath which he clasped the child, saying in a low voice:

"Come, my soul, come, mine eyes! Come, my little heart! Come, and put on the baptismal robe."

He carried away the child pressed to his breast. Being timid, and yet curious, Thaïs, with her head outside the cloak, clasped her hands around her friend's neck as he carried her out into the darkness. They went along dark lanes; traversed the Jewish quarter; and passed a cemetery, from which the sinister cry of an osprey proceeded. They passed at the crossroads beneath crosses, upon which hung the bodies of executed criminals, upon whose arms croaking ravens were perched. Thaïs hid her head in the slave's breast. She dare not look again during the rest of the journey. Suddenly it seemed to her as if they were descending underground. When she opened her eyes she found herself in a narrow cave, lit by resin torches, the walls of which were covered with great upright covered figures, which appeared animate in the smoke. There were men, clad in long tunics, bearing palms in the midst of lambs, doves, and vine branches.

Among these figures Thaïs recognized Jesus of Nazareth, because anemones blossomed at his feet. In the midst of the hall, near a great stone font full of water to the brim, stood an old man with a miter on his head, clad in a scarlet dalmatica embroidered with gold. His heavily bearded face had a soft and gentle expression, in spite of his rich costume. He was Bishop Vivantius, who though an exiled Prince of the Church of Cyrene, gained his living as a weaver by making coarse goat's hair stuff. Two poor children stood upright at his side. Close by stood an old negress with a small white robe in her hand. Ahmes, after putting down the child, knelt before the Bishop and said:

"Father, here is the little soul, the daughter of my own soul. I bring her to you so that, according to your promise, if it seems good to you, you may give her the baptism of life."

At these words the Bishop, stretching out his arms, displayed his mutilated hands. He had had his fingers torn for confessing the faith in the days of trial. Thaïs was afraid, and fled into the arms of Ahmes. But the priest reassured her with caressing words.

"Fear nothing, beloved. You have here a spiritual father in Ahmes, who is called Theodore among the faithful, and a gentle mother in grace, who has prepared for you a white robe with her own hands." Turning towards the negress, he added: "Her name is Nitida; she is a slave on this earth. But Jesus, in heaven, will take her as his bride." Then he asked the young neophyte: "Thaïs, do you believe in God, the omnipotent Father, in his only Son who died for our salvation, and in all that the apostles teach?"

"Yes," replied the negro and negress, who were holding her hands.

Following the Bishop's instructions, Nitida knelt down and stripped Thaïs of all her clothing. The child was naked, save for a charm about her neck. The Bishop dipped her three times in the baptismal font. The acolytes presented the oil with which Vivantius anointed her, and the salt, a grain of which he placed upon the lips of the catechumen. Then after drying this body, which was destined after many trials for eternal life, Nitida dressed her in the white robe she had herself woven.

The Bishop gave all of them the kiss of peace, and at the conclusion of the ceremony removed his sacerdotal ornaments.

When they were all outside the crypt, Ahmes said:

"We must rejoice to-day because we have given a soul to the Lord; let us go to your house, Pastor Vivantius, and give ourselves up to joy for the rest of the night."

"You have spoken the truth, Theodore," replied the Bishop.

He led the little party to his house, which was quite near. It consisted of a single chamber furnished with two looms, a large table and a well-worn carpet. As soon as they entered, the Nubian said:

"Nitida, bring the pan and jar of oil and let us make a good meal."

As he spoke, he drew from beneath his cloak some small fish he had hidden there; then, lighting a large fire, he began to cook them. The Bishop, the child, the two boys and the two slaves sat down in a circle upon the floor, and ate the fish, blessing God as they did so.

Vivantius spoke of the martyrdom he had suffered, and

announced the Church's approaching triumph. His language was rough, but full of simile. He compared the life of the just to a purple cloth, and to explain baptism, he said:

"The Holy Spirit floated on the waters, for which reason Christians receive the baptism of water. But demons also dwell in streams: fountains consecrated to nymphs are to be feared, and we see that certain waters occasion different maladies of soul and body."

Sometimes, too, he expressed himself in enigma, and thus inspired the child with profound admiration. At the end of the meal he offered a little wine to his guests, whose tongues it loosened so that they began to sing litanies and chants. Ahmes and Nitida rose and danced a Nubian dance which they had learnt as children, and which, without a doubt, had been danced in their tribe since the beginning of the world. It was a dance of love; moving the arms and body in rhythm, they feigned alternately to flee and follow. They rolled their eyes, and showed their glistening teeth when they smiled.

In this way Thaïs received the Holy Baptism.

She loved amusement, and as she grew vague desires were born in her. She danced and sang all day with wandering children of the streets, and at night returned to her father's house still singing.

But she preferred the society of boys and girls to that of gentle Ahmes. She did not notice that her friend was less often with her. Persecution having ceased the assemblies of the Christians became more regular, and the Nubian always attended. His zeal became hotter; sometimes mysterious menaces escaped his lips. He said that the rich would not keep their wealth. He went to those public places where humble Christians were wont to assemble, and there collected the wretches stretched out in the shade of the walls, and announced to them the freeing of slaves and the near approach of Justice.

"In the realm of God," he said, "slaves shall drink fresh

wine and eat delicious fruits, while the rich shall be at their feet like dogs, and devour the crumbs from their table."

These ideas did not remain secret: they were published abroad in the city, and masters feared lest Ahmes should excite their slaves to revolt. The innkeeper, too, had a profound hatred for him, which he carefully dissimulated.

One day a silver saltcellar, reserved for the table of the gods, disappeared from the inn. Ahmes was accused of stealing it, as a mark of hatred against his master and the gods of the empire. The accusation was entirely without proof, and the slave denied it with all his strength. None the less he was taken before the Tribunal, and, as he was supposed to be a worthless slave, the judge condemned him to death.

"Your hands," the judge said to him, "of which you have not made good use, shall be nailed to a cross."

Ahmes listened quietly to this sentence, saluted the judge with great respect, and was led away to the public prison. During the three days he was confined there he never ceased to preach the Gospel to the prisoners, and it has since been said that criminals, and even the jailor himself, touched by his words, believed in Christ crucified.

He was led to those crossroads which one night, less than two years before, he had quickly passed bearing beneath his white cloak his well-beloved flower Thaïs, the daughter of his soul. When his hands were nailed to the cross he uttered not even a groan, only several times he said: "I am thirsty!"

His penalty lasted three days and three nights. It is hardly possible to believe that human flesh could endure such lengthy torture. Several times he appeared to be dead; the flies devoured part of his eyes; but suddenly he would raise his bleeding eyelids. On the morning of the fourth day he smiled and said:

"Here are the angels of God! They bring me wine and fruit. How fresh is the beating of their wings!"

He expired.

In death his face retained an expression of happy ecstasy. The soldiers who guarded the cross were filled with admiration. Vivantius, accompanied by a few of his fellow Christians, came to claim the body for burial among the remains of the martyrs in the crypt of St. John the Baptist. The Church guarded in veneration the memory of St. Theodore the Nubian.

Three years later Constantine, the conqueror of Maxentius, published an edict in which he assured the Christians peace, and from that time the faithful were only persecuted by heretics.

Thaïs was eleven years old when her friend was tortured to death. She felt sorrow and invincible fear. Her soul was not sufficiently pure to understand that Ahmes, by his life and death, was a happy man. The idea sprung up in her little soul that it was only possible to be good in this world at the expense of frightful suffering. She feared to be good, for her delicate flesh feared to suffer.

Before she came of age she had lovers in the boys of the harbor, and she followed the old men, who wandered in the evening in the outskirts of the city; with the money she received she bought herself jewels and clothing.

As she did not take home any of the money she earned, her mother ill treated her. To avoid her mother's blows she fled with bare feet to the ramparts of the city, where she hid among the lizards in clefts of the stones. There she thought in envy of the richly dressed women in their litters surrounded by slaves.

One day, after being beaten more than usual, she was crouching near the gate, when an old woman stopped in front of her, looked at her for some seconds, and then said:

"O pretty flower! lovely child! Happy is the father who begat you and the mother who brought you into the world!"

Thaïs remained silent, with her eyes fixed upon the ground. Her eyes were red and showed she had been crying.

"My white violet," said the old woman, "is not your mother fortunate to have nursed a little goddess like you, and does not your father rejoice over you at the bottom of his heart?"

Then the child, as if speaking to herself, said: "My father is a drunkard and my mother is a miser."

The old woman looked to right and left to be sure that no one was watching her. Then in a caressing voice she said:

"Sweet hyacinth, come with me, and your life shall be a continuous dance and smile. I will feed you with honeycomb, and my son, my own son, will love you as his own eyes. My son is beautiful, he is young; he has only a light beard upon his chin; his skin is soft."

Thaïs replied: "I will go with you."

Getting up, she followed the old woman out of the city.

This woman, whose name was Moeroe, took from place to place girls and boys whom she taught to dance and afterwards hired out to the rich to appear at feasts.

Seeing that Thaïs would soon become the most beautiful of women, she taught her music by means of a whip, and lashed her legs with leather thongs when they did not rise in time with the cithara. Her son, who was a decrepit abortion, ageless and unsexed, ill treated this girl, as if he were pursuing in her the entire female race with his hatred. Being a rival of the dancers, whose grace he affected, he taught Thaïs the art of simulating the pantomime, by expression of face, gesture and attitude, all human sentiments, and especially the passions of love. He, as if in disgust, gave her the advice of a skilled master; but, jealous of his pupil, he scratched her cheeks, pinched her arms, or pricked her from behind with a needle, as naughty girls do, when he saw too clearly that she was born for the pleasure of men. Thanks to these lessons, she became in a short time a musician, pantomime and an excellent dancer. The harshness of her master did not surprise her, for it seemed natural to her to be ill-treated. She even felt a certain amount of respect for the old woman, who was a musician, and drank Greek wine. Moeroe, when staying at Antioch for a time, hired her pupil as dancer and flute player to the rich business men of the city, who were giving feasts. Thaïs danced and pleased. The most vulgar bankers took her, after leaving the table, to the groves of the Orontes. She gave herself to all without knowing the price of love. But one night, after dancing before the most elegant young men in the city, the son of the Proconsul approached her, glowing with youth and pleasure, and said to her in a voice which seemed moist with kisses:

"Why, Thaïs, am I not the crown which surrounds your hair, the tunic which presses upon your charming body, the sandal of your beautiful foot! I desire you to tread on me with your feet like a sandal; I desire my caresses to be your tunic and your crown. Come, lovely child, come to my home and forget the world."

She looked at him as he spoke, and saw that he was beautiful. Suddenly she felt the sweat standing on her forehead; she became green as the grass; she staggered—a cloud descended before her eyes. But she refused to follow him. His ardent looks and words of love were all in vain, and when he took her in his arms to force her she roughly repulsed him. Then he became a new, unknown and invincible power, she resisted:

"What folly!" said the guests. "Lollius is noble; he is good-looking and rich, and yet a flute player disdains him."

Lollius returned home alone, and during the night became eaten up with love. In the morning he went, pale and red-eyed, and hung flowers upon the flute player's door. But Thaïs, seized with trouble and affright, shunned him. She suffered and did not know her malady. She asked herself why she had thus changed and whence her melancholy came. She repulsed all her lovers; they became horrible to her. She did not want to see the light, and remained all day reclining on her bed, sobbing with her head in the pillows. Lollius found out a means of forcing her door, and came many times to supplicate and curse this wayward child. She remained in his presence as fearful as a maiden, and repeated:

"I will not! I will not!"

Then at the end of a fortnight she knew she loved him; she followed him to his home and did not leave him. Theirs was a delicious life. They spent the day gazing into each other's eyes, and speaking to each other in the way that children do. In the evenings they walked along the lonely banks of the Orontes, and lost themselves in the laurel woods. Sometimes they rose at dawn to go and gather hyacinths upon the slopes of the Silpicus. They drank out of the same cup, and when she raised a grape to her mouth, he took it with his lips from between her lips.

Moeroe came in great indignation to the house of Lollius to reclaim Thaïs.

"She is my daughter," said she, "whom you have taken from me, my perfumed flower, flesh of my flesh!"

Lollius sent her away with a large sum of money. But as she returned, demanding still more golden staters, the young man had her imprisoned, and as the magistrates discovered several crimes of which she was guilty, she was condemned to death, and given to the wild beasts.

Thaïs loved Lollius with all the fury of her imagination and surprise of her innocence. She said to him from the bottom of her heart:

"I have always been yours."

Lollius replied to her:

"You are like no other woman."

The charm lasted for six months, and was broken in one day. Suddenly Thaïs felt herself to be alone and empty. She no longer recognized Lollius, she thought:

"What has changed him thus in a moment? How is it that he is like all other men and no longer like himself?"

She left him, not without a secret desire to find Lollius in another, since she could no longer find him in himself. She thought, too, that life with a person whom she had never loved would be less sad than with a person whom she no longer loved. She showed herself in the company of rich pleasure seekers at those sacred fêtes where choirs of naked females danced in the temples, and troops of courtesans swam across the Orontes. She took part in all the pleasures which the elegant monstrous city provided; she in particular frequented the theaters, in which skilled pantomimes from every land appeared amid the applause of a spectacle-loving audience.

She carefully observed the pantomimes, dancers, actresses, and particularly the women who represented the goddess-lovers of young men and the mortals loved by the gods in the tragedies. After discovering the secrets by which they charmed the crowd she told herself, as she was more beautiful than they, she could act still better. She went to the chief of the pantomimes and asked to be allowed to join his troop. Thanks to her beauty and the lessons she had received from old Moeroe, she was admitted, and appeared upon the stage as Dirce.

She had but a moderate success, as she lacked experience, and as the spectators had not been excited to admiration by constant praise being showered upon her. But after a few months of obscure parts the power of her beauty burst upon the stage with such force that the whole city was moved. All Antioch crowded to the theater. The Imperial magistrates and chief citizens went there, driven by the force of opinion. The porters, sweepers and workmen deprived themselves of garlic and bread to pay for their seats. Poets composed epigrams in her honor. Bearded philosophers declaimed against her at the bath and school when her litter passed. Christian priests turned their heads. The threshold of her house was crowned with flowers and sprinkled with blood. She received from her lovers untold gold, and all the treasures amassed by the careful old men flowed like rivers to her feet. Therefore her soul was happy. She rejoiced in peaceful pride at public favor and the goodness of the gods, and being loved so much by others she loved herself.

After enjoying for some years the admiration and love of Antioch, she had a desire to revisit Alexandria and show her glory to the city in which, as a child, she wandered in misery and shame, famished and thin as a grasshopper in the middle of a dusty road. The golden city received her with joy and showered more wealth upon her. Her appearance at the games was a triumph. Innumerable admirers and lovers came to her. She received them carelessly, for at last she despaired of recovering Lollius.

She received among many others the philosopher Nicias, although he professed to live without desire. In spite of his wealth, he was intelligent and gentle. But he did not charm her with his wonderful wisdom or the grace of his senti-ments. She did not love him, and was sometimes even irri-tated by his delicate irony. He wounded her by his perpetual doubt. He believed in nothing, she in everything. She be-lieved in divine providence, the omnipotence of evil spirits, fate, incantation and eternal justice. She believed in Jesus Christ, and in the good goddess of the Syrians; she believed, too, that dogs barked when black Hecate passed the cross-ways, and that a woman could inspire love by pouring a philter into a cup containing a sheep's bleeding fleece. She thirsted for the unknown, she called nameless beings, and lived in perpetual expectancy. The future frightened her and she desired knowledge of it. She surrounded herself with priests of Isis, Chaldean magicians, witch doctors and sor-cerers, who always deceived but never left her. She feared death, and saw it everywhere. When she yielded to pleasure, it seemed to her as if an ice-cold finger touched her naked shoulder, and, turning pale, she shrieked in terror.

"What does it matter, Thaïs," Nicias said to her, "if our

destiny is to descend with white hair and wasted cheeks to
eternal Night, or this day, now smiling in the sunny sky,
is to be our last? Let us taste life! We shall live long if we
feel much. There is no other intelligence than that of the
senses: love is understanding. That of which we are ignorant is not. What is the use of tormenting ourselves for
naught?"

She answered him angrily:

"I despise those who, like you, neither hope nor fear. I
desire knowledge! I desire knowledge!"

To discover the secret of life she began to read books of
philosophy, but she did not understand them. The further the
years of her infancy passed from her, the more willingly she
recalled them to her mind. She loved to traverse in disguise
the lanes, banks and public places where she had grown up
in misery. She regretted the loss of her parents, and particularly the fact of never having loved them. When she met
Christian priests, she thought of her baptism and felt
troubled. One night when, enveloped in a long cloak, with
her blonde hair hidden beneath a dark hood, she was wandering as usual in the suburbs of the city, she found herself, without knowing why, before the poor church of St. John the
Baptist. She heard singing within, and saw a brilliant light
shining through the cracks of the door. There was nothing
strange in this, as for twenty years the Christians, protected
by the conquerors of Maxentius, had solemnized their feasts
in public.

But these chants signified an ardent appeal to the soul. The
actress pushed open the door with her hand, and entered as
a guest at the mysteries. She found a numerous assembly,
women, children, and old men, kneeling before a tomb against
the wall. This tomb was simply a stone font, with some
branches and grapes roughly carved upon it; it had, however,
received great honor: it was covered with green palms and
crowned with red roses. All around innumerable lights shone
out of the shadow, in which the smoke of Arabian gums

seemed like the folds of angels' robes. On the wall were figures like visions from heaven. Priests clad in white lay prostrate at the foot of the sarcophagus. The hymn which these priests and people were chanting expressed the delights of suffering, and mingled in a triumphal mourning so much joy with so much grief, that Thaïs while listening to them felt the pleasures of life and the terrors of death run side by side through her reviving senses.

When they had finished singing, the faithful rose to go and kiss one by one, the side of the tomb. They were simple men, accustomed to manual work. They advanced with heavy tread, set eyes and drooping mouth, with an air of candor. They knelt in turn before the sarcophagus and pressed their lips to it. The women lifted in their arms the little children and placed their cheeks gently against the stone. Thaïs, surprised and disturbed, asked a deacon why they did this.

"Do you know, woman," replied the deacon, "that to-day we celebrate the blessed memory of St. Theodore the Nubian, who suffered for the faith in the days of the Emperor Diocletian? He lived a chaste life and died a martyr; that is why, clad in white, we bear red roses to his glorious tomb."

On hearing this Thaïs fell on her knees and burst into tears. The half extinct recollection of Ahmes awoke in her mind. Upon this obscure memory, gentle and painful as it was, the light of the tapers, the perfume of the roses, the clouds of incense, the harmony of the chants, and the piety of the congregation threw the charms of glory. Thaïs thought:

"He was good, and here he is great and beautiful! How high above men he is uplifted! What, then, is this unknown thing, which is worth more than wealth and pleasure?"

She rose slowly and turned towards the tomb of the Saint, who had loved her violet eyes, in which tears glistened in the taper's light; then, with bent head, humble and slow, last of all, with the lips on which so much desire had rested, she kissed the slave's tomb.

Returning to her house, she found Nicias waiting with

perfumed hair and unfastened tunic, and reading a treatise on morality. He advanced to meet her with open arms.

"Naughty Thaïs," cried he, with laughter in his voice, "while you delayed coming, do you know what I found in this manuscript written by the gravest of the Stoics? Precepts of virtue and maxims of pride? No! upon the austere papyrus I saw thousands of little Thaïses. They were each as high as a finger, and yet their grace was infinite and all were the one Thaïs. Some dragged behind them cloaks of purple and gold; others, like a white cloud, floated in the air under diaphanous veils. Others, motionless and divine in their nudity, expressed no thought, the better to inspire pleasure. Last of all were two hand in hand, so much alike that it was impossible to distinguish one from the other. They both smiled; the first said: 'I am love'; the other: 'I am death.'"

As he said this he clasped Thaïs in his arms, and without seeing the fierce glance she fixed upon the ground, he added one thought to another careless that they were thrown away upon her.

"Yes, when I was reading the line which says: 'Nothing must turn you aside from training your soul,' I read: 'The kisses of Thaïs are more ardent than flames and sweeter than honey.' That is the way in which, through your fault, naughty child, a philosopher to-day understands works of philosophy. It is true that, all that we are, we discover our own thoughts only in those of other people, and read the books, like the one I have just been reading, a little. . . ."

She was not listening, and her mind was still before the Nubian's tomb. As he heard her sigh he kissed her, and said:

"Be not sad, my child. The only happiness in this world is to forget it. We have secrets for that. Come, let us deceive life; it is well worth deceiving. Come! Let us love."

She repulsed him crying:

"Love! You have never loved anyone. I do not love you! No, I do not love you! I hate you! Go away! I hate you!

I hate and despise all the happy and the rich! Go away!
Go away! . . . There is no goodness except in the unfortunate. When I was a child, I knew a black slave who was
crucified. He was good; he was full of love, and he possessed
the secret of life. You would not be worthy to wash his
feet. Go away! I will see you no more."

She stretched herself, face downwards, upon the floor and
passed the night in sobs, resolving henceforth to live like St.
Theodore in poverty and simplicity.

On the morrow she returned to the pleasures she had
arranged. As she knew her still immaculate beauty would not
last long, she made haste to obtain all possible joy and glory
from it. At the theater, where she performed with more care
than ever, she brought to life the imaginations of sculptors,
painters, and poets. Recognizing in the form, attitude, movements and gait of the actress an idea of the divine harmony
which rules the world, savants and philosophers put so perfect
a grace among the virtues, and said: "Thaïs is a mathematician." The ignorant, poor, humble and timid, before whom
she consented to appear, blessed her for her celestial charity.
Still she was sad in the midst of praise, and more than ever
feared to die. Nothing could dispel her uneasiness, not even
her house and gardens, which were so celebrated as to be pro-
verbial in the city.

She had planted trees, brought at great expense from India
and Persia. A running stream irrigated them, and ruined
colonnades, wild rocks, imitated by a skilful architect, were
reflected in a lake in which statues gazed at their own reflection. In the midst of the garden stood the Nymphs' grotto,
which owed its name to three great waxen female figures
which stood upon the threshold. These women were undress-
ing themselves to take a bath. They turned their heads
uneasily for fear of being seen, and appeared to be alive.
Light only entered this retreat across the small sheets of water,
which softened and colored it. From the walls on all sides

hung, as in the sacred grotto, crowns, garlands and votive pictures in which the beauty of Thaïs was celebrated. There were, too, tragic and comic masks in bright colors, pictures representing either scenes in the theater, grotesque figures, or fabulous animals. In the middle stood upon a column a little ivory Eros, of ancient and wonderful workmanship. It was a gift from Nicias. A black marble she goat stood in a hollow, from which its shining agate eyes could be seen. Six alabaster kids crowded around its teats; but raising its wild feet and flat head it seemed impatient to scramble among the rocks. The earth was covered with Byzantine tapestry, pillows embroidered by the yellow men of Cathay and the skins of Lybian lions. Pans of perfume smoked imperceptibly. At the back of all, in the purple shadow, shone golden nails on the shell of a great Indian tortoise, which, reversed, served as the great actress's bed. There each day, to the murmur of the waters, among the perfume and flowers, Thaïs reclined in comfort, and while awaiting supper time talked with her friends or simply thought, either of the business of the theater, or the flight of years.

On this day she was resting after the theater in the Nymphs' grotto. She was looking in her mirror for the first signs of her beauty's decline, and thinking with fear that the time of white hair and wrinkles would come. In vain she tried to reassure herself by saying that the burning of certain herbs to the words of a magic formula would be sufficient to bring back her freshness. A pitiless voice cried out:

"You will grow old, Thaïs, you will grow old!"

The sweat of fear froze upon her forehead. Then as she looked once more tenderly in her mirror and found herself still beautiful and worthy of love, smiling to herself, she murmured: "There is not in Alexandria a single woman who can compare with me in suppleness of figure, grace of movement, and magnificence of arms, and the arms, O my mirror, are the true chains of love!"

As she thought thus she saw an unknown standing before her, with burning eyes and unkempt beard, and clad in a richly broidered robe. Dropping her mirror, she screamed out in affright.

Paphnutius stood motionless, and, seeing her beauty, in the bottom of his soul offered up this prayer:

"O God, grant that this woman's face, instead of scandalizing, may edify thy servant."

Then, forcing himself to speak, he said:

"Thaïs, I dwell in a far-off land, and the renown of your beauty has led me to you. Report says that you are the most skilful of actresses and the most irresistible of women. The tales of your wealth and your loves seem fabulous, and recall Rhodopis of old, whose wonderful history all the boatmen of the Nile knew by heart. Therefore I have been seized with a desire to know you, and I see that the truth even exceeds the report. You are a thousand times wiser and more beautiful than you are reported. And now that I see you, I say to myself, 'It is impossible to approach her without staggering like a drunken man.' "

These were mocking words; but the monk, animated with pious zeal, uttered them with real ardor. But Thaïs looked without displeasure upon this strange being who had made her afraid. Paphnutius astonished her by his rough and savage appearance and his somber glances charged with fire. She was curious to know the state and life of a man so different from all she knew. She replied, gently mocking him:

"You seem quick to admire, stranger. Take care my looks do not consume you to the bone! Take care to love me!"

He said to her:

"I love you, Thaïs! I love you more than my life and more than myself. For you I have left my dear desert; for you my lips, vowed to silence, have spoken profane words; for you I have seen what I ought not to have seen, I have heard what I was forbidden to hear; for you my soul is troubled, my heart is open and thoughts have gushed out from it, like the running streams at which doves drink; for you I have walked day and night across the sands of the desert peopled with worms and vampires; for you I have put my naked foot on vipers and scorpions! Yes, I love you, not as those men who, inflamed with carnal desire, come to you as devouring wolves or raging bulls. You are dear to them as the gazelle is to the lion. Their carnal love is devouring your soul, woman! I love you in spirit and in truth, I love you in God for ever and ever; the feeling in my breast for you is called real ardor and divine charity. I promise you something better than flowery drunkenness and the dreams of a brief night. I promise you holy love feasts and celestial marriage. The felicity I bring you will never end; it is unthinkable; it is ineffable, and such that, if those who are fortunate in this world could only see a shadow of it, they would immediately die of astonishment."

Thaïs laughed with the air of an unbeliever.

"Friend," said she, "show me this marvelous love. Hasten; too long speeches injure my beauty, do not lose a moment! I am impatient to know this happiness you announce; but, to tell you the truth, I am afraid that I shall never know it, and that your promise will end in mere words. It is easier to promise a great happiness than to give it. Each has his talent. I believe yours is discovery. You speak of an unknown love. So long have kisses been exchanged that it would be very extraordinary were there still any love secrets. On this subject lovers know more than magicians."

"Thaïs, do not mock. I am bringing you the unknown love."

"Friend, you are late. I know all love."

"The love I bring you is full of glory, while the loves you know are born in shame."

Thaïs looked at him with an angry expression, and a hard line across her little forehead.

"You are bold, stranger, to offend your hostess. Look at

me, and tell me if I resemble a creature of shame. No! I am
not ashamed, nor all those who live as I do, although they
may be less beautiful and rich than I. I have sown pleasure in
all my steps, and for that I am known throughout the world.
I have more power than the masters of the world. I have
seen them at my feet. Look at me, look at these little feet;
thousands of men would pay with their blood for the pleasure of kissing them. I am not very great and do not hold
much of a place upon earth. To those who see me from the
top of the Serapeum when I pass in the street, I resemble a
grain of rice; but this grain of rice among men has caused
mourning, despair, hate and crimes enough to fill Tartarus.
Am I not mad to speak of shame, when everything around
me shouts of glory?"

"Glory in men's eyes is infamy before God. Woman, we
have been nursed in countries so different that it is not surprising that neither our language nor our thoughts are the
same. But heaven is my witness that I desire to agree with
you, and my plan is not to leave you until our sentiments are
the same. Who will inspire me with burning words, which
shall make you melt like wax at my breath, woman, and
allow the fingers of my desire to model you according to
their taste? What virtue will deliver you to me, O dearest
of souls, so that the spirit animating me may create you a
second time, impress a new beauty upon you, and make you
cry in tears of joy: 'To-day, indeed, is the day of my birth!'
Who will make a fountain of Siloe flow from my heart, in
which, after bathing, you shall find your primal purity? Who
will change me into a Jordan, whose waters, overflowing you,
shall give you eternal life?"

Thaïs was angry no more.

"This man," she thought, "speaks of eternal life, and all he
says seems written upon a talisman. There is no doubt that he
is a magician, and has secrets against old age and death."

She resolved to offer herself to him; so, feigning to fear

him, she stepped back some paces, and, retiring to the back of the grotto, sat down upon the edge of the bed, skilfully replacing her tunic upon her breast, and then, motionless and mute, she waited with downcast eyes. Her long lashes cast a gentle shadow on her cheeks. Her attitude expressed shame; her naked feet hung down, and she resembled a dreaming child sitting upon the bank of a river.

But Paphnutius looked at her, and did not move. His trembling knees could no longer support him; his tongue was parched in his mouth; a frightful tumult arose in his brain. Suddenly his look was veiled, and he saw before him nothing but a thick cloud. He thought that the hand of Jesus had been placed before his eyes to conceal the woman from him. Reassured by such aid as this, made strong, and fortified, he said, with a gravity worthy of a hermit of the desert:

"If you give yourself to me do you think you will be concealed from God?"

She shook her head.

"God! who forces him always to have his eye upon the Nymphs' grotto? Let him retire if we offend him! But why should we offend him? Since he has created us he can be neither angry nor surprised to see us such as he has made us, and acting according to the nature he has given us. Too much is often said for him, and ideas borrowed which he has never had. Know his real character? Who are you to speak to me in his name?"

At the question the monk, half opening his borrowed garment, showed his robe and said:

"I am Paphnutius, priest of Antinöe, and I come from the holy desert. The land which took away Abraham from Chaldæa and Lot from Sodom has separated me from the world. I exist no more for men. But your image appeared to me in my Jerusalem of sand, and I knew that you were full of corruption and that in you was death. Here am I before you, woman, as before a sepulcher, and I cry: 'Thaïs, arise.' "

At the name of Paphnutius, and the words monk and priest, she had paled in fear. Then, her hair disheveled, she crawled with clasped hands to the holy man's feet, weeping and groaning:

"Do me no ill! Why have you come? What do you desire? Do me no ill! I know that the holy men of the desert detest the women who, like myself, are made to please. I am afraid you hate me, and wish to injure me. Go! I do not doubt your power; but understand, Paphnutius, you must neither despise nor hate me. I have never, like so many men I know, laughed at your willing poverty. In your turn do not make my wealth a crime. I am beautiful, and a clever actress. I have no more chosen my condition than I have my nature. I was made for what I am. I was born to charm men. But you just now said you loved me. Do not use your science against me. Do not pronounce magic words which will destroy my beauty or change me into a pillar of salt. Do not frighten me! I am already very much afraid. Do not make me die! I fear death so much."

He signed to her to rise, and said:

"Child, be reassured. I will not treat you with hatred and contempt. I come to you on behalf of him who, sitting on the borders of the well, drank from the pitcher which the Samaritan woman offered him, and who, when he supped at Simon's house, received perfumes from Mary. I am not sinless that I may throw the first stone at you. I have often ill employed the abundant graces God has given me. It is not anger; it is pity which has taken me by the hand to lead me to you. I have been able, without lying, to approach you with words of love, for it is the zeal of my heart which led me to you. I am consumed with the fire of charity, and if your eyes, accustomed to the gross spectacles of the flesh, could see things in their mystic aspect, I should appear to you as a branch torn from the burning bush, which God showed on the mountain to Moses, to make him understand true love—

that love which inflames without consuming us, and which, far from leaving behind it embers and ashes, embalms and perfumes for ever all it penetrates."

"Monk, I believe you, and no longer fear snare or hurt from you. I have often heard tell of the hermits of the Thebaid. The stories I have heard of the lives of Anthony and Paul are marvelous. Your name was not unknown to me, and I have been told that, though still young, you equal in virtue the oldest Anchorite. From what I saw of you, without knowing who you were, I felt you were not an ordinary man. Tell me, can you do for me what neither the priests of Isis, the priests of Hermes, the priests of Celestial Juno, the Chaldean magicians, nor the Babylonian sorcerers can do? Monk, if you love me, can you prevent me from dying?"

"Woman, those will live who wish to live. Shun the abominable delights in which are eternal death. Snatch from the demons, who would dreadfully burn it, the body which God made and animated with his breath. Consumed with fatigue as you are, come and refresh yourself at the blessed springs of solitude; come and drink at those fountains concealed in the desert, which flow from heaven. Anxious soul, at last come and possess your desire! Heart, greedy of joy, come and taste real joy, poverty, renunciation, self-oblivion, abandonment of the whole being in God's breast. Enemy of the Christ, and to-morrow his well-beloved, come to him. Come, you who sought, and you shall say, 'I have found love!'"

But Thaïs seemed to contemplate things afar off:

"Monk," asked she, "if I renounce my pleasures and do penitence, is it true that I shall be born again in heaven, with my body intact in all its beauty?"

"Thaïs, I bring you eternal life. Believe me, for what I announce is true."

"Who guarantees me that it is true?"

"David and the prophets, the Scriptures and the marvels which you shall witness."

"Monk, I would believe you. For I admit I have not found happiness in this world. My lot was better than a queen's, and yet life has brought me much sorrow and suffering, and I am infinitely weary of it. All women envy my destiny, and I sometimes envy the lot of the old toothless woman who, when I was little, sold honeycomb at the City gate. The idea has come to me many times that only the poor are good, happy and blessed, and that there is a great solace in lowly and humble life. Monk, you have removed the billows from my soul and made rise to the surface that which slept at the bottom. What am I to believe, alas! and what shall I become, and what is life?"

While she spoke thus, Paphnutius was transfigured; a celestial joy spread over his face.

"Listen," said he, "I have not entered your dwelling alone. Another accompanied me, another is standing here at my side. Him you cannot see, because your eyes are still unworthy to contemplate him; but soon you will see him in his charming splendor and say: 'he alone is lovable!' Just now, if he had not placed his soft hand over my eyes, Thaïs, I should perhaps have committed sin with you, for I am myself but weakness and trouble. But he has saved both of us; he is as good as he is powerful, and his name is Saviour. He was promised to the world by David and the Sibyl, adored in his cradle by the shepherds and magicians, crucified by the Pharisees, buried by the holy women, revealed to the world by the apostles, and attested by the martyrs. Learning that you fear death, woman, I am here in your house come to prevent you from death! Didst thou not, Jesus, appear to me at that moment, as thou appearedst to the men of Galilee in those days of wonder, when the stars, descending with thee from heaven, were so near the earth that the holy innocents could

seize them in their hands as they played in their mothers'
arms upon the terraces of Bethlehem? Are we not, Jesus, in
thy company, and art thou not showing us the reality of thy
precious body? Is not thy face there and the tear running
down thy cheek a real tear? Yes, the angel of eternal justice
will receive it, and it shall be the ransom for the soul of Thaïs.
Art thou not there, Jesus? Thy adorable lips are open. Thou
canst speak; speak, I am listening. And you, Thaïs, happy
Thaïs, listen to what the Saviour himself says to you; he
speaks, not I. He says: 'I have sought you long, my wandering sheep! I have found you at last. Fly from me no more.
Take my hands, poor little one, and I will bear you on my
shoulders to the heavenly fold. Come, Thaïs, come, my elect,
come and weep with me!' "

Paphnutius fell on his knees in ecstasy.

Then Thaïs saw upon his face the reflection of the living
Jesus.

"O past days of my childhood!" she said through her sobs,
"O my gentle father Ahmes, good St. Theodore, why had I
not died in your white robe while you carried me away in the
dawn, fresh from the baptismal water!"

Paphnutius sprang toward her, saying:

"You are baptized! . . . O divine wisdom! O Providence!
O good God! I now know the power which attracted me
towards you. I know what rendered you so dear and beautiful in my eyes. It is the virtue of the baptismal water, which
made me leave the shadow of God, where I lived, to seek you
in the poisoned atmosphere of the world. A drop, doubtless,
of the water which baptized your body, splashed upon my
forehead. Come, my sister, and receive from your brother
the kiss of peace."

The monk placed his lips upon the courtesan's forehead.

Then he became silent, leaving God to speak, and there
was no sound in the Nymphs' grotto but the sobs of Thaïs
mingled with the song of the running water.

She wept without drying her tears, when her black slave came in laden with stuffs, perfumes, and garlands.

"It is scarcely right to weep," said she, trying to smile. "Tears sodden the eyes and spoil their tint. I must sup to-night with friends, and I desire to be beautiful, for there will be women there who will notice my tired face. These slaves come to dress me. Retire, my father, and let them do so. They are skilled and adroit; so I had to pay very dearly for them. Look at this one who has large golden rings and shows her white teeth. Her I bought from the Proconsul's wife."

Paphnutius at first thought of opposing with all his might the idea of Thaïs going to this supper. But, determined to act prudently, he asked whom she would meet there.

She replied that she would see the host, old Cotta, prefect of the fleet, Nicias, and several other philosophers, the poet Callicrates, the high priest of Serapis, rich young men especially interested in horse-breeding, and lastly, women about whom nothing could be said, and whose youth was their only virtue.

Then, by a supernatural inspiration:

"Go among them, Thaïs," said the monk; "go! But I will not leave you. I will go with you to this feast, and sit silently at your side."

She burst out laughing. And while the two slaves busied themselves around her, she said:

"What will they say when they see that I have a monk of the Thebaid for a lover?"

THE BANQUET

WHEN, followed by Paphnutius, Thaïs entered the banqueting hall, the guests were, for the most part, already reclining upon couches before the horseshoe-shaped table, covered with glistening plate. In the center of the table was a silver basin, surmounted by four Satyrs inclining leathern bottles, from which flowed upon boiled fish the sauce in which they swam. At the appearance of Thaïs acclamations arose from all sides.

"Greeting to the sister of Charites!"

"Greeting to the silent Melpomene, whose glances can express everything!"

"Greeting to the well beloved of gods and men!"

"To the greatly desired one!"

"To her who gives suffering and its cure!"

"To the pearl of Racotes!"

"To the rose of Alexandria!"

She waited impatiently till this torrent of praise had ceased; and then she said to Cotta, her host:

"Lucius, I have brought you a monk of the desert, Paphnutius, priest of Antinöe; he is a holy man, whose words burn like fire."

Lucius Aurelius Cotta, prefect of the fleet, rose, saying:

"Welcome, Paphnutius, you who profess the Christian faith. I have respect for a cult, henceforth imperial. The divine Constantine placed your co-religionists in the front rank of the Empire's friends. Latin wisdom, in fact, ought to admit your Christ into our Pantheon. There is a maxim of our fathers which says that every god has something divine in him. But let us leave that. Let us drink and be glad while there is yet time."

Old Cotta said this with serenity. He had just been studying the model of a new galley and completing the sixth volume of his history of the Carthaginians. Sure that he had not wasted the day, he was content with himself and the gods.

"Paphnutius, you see here several men worthy of love. Hermodorus, High Priest of Serapis, the philosopher Dorion, Nicias and Zenothemis, the poet Callicrates, young Chereas and Aristobulus, both sons of a dear comrade of my youth; and near them are Philinna and Drosea, who must be greatly admired for their beauty."

Nicias embraced Paphnutius, and said in his ear:

"I warned you, my friend, that Venus was powerful. Her gentle violence has brought you here in spite of yourself. Listen, you are a very pious man, but if you do not recognize her as the mother of the gods, your ruin is certain. The old mathematician Melanthus used to say: 'I could not demonstrate the properties of a triangle without the aid of Venus.' "

Dorion, who for some minutes had been looking at the newcomer, suddenly clapped his hands and uttered cries of admiration.

"It is he, friends! His look, his beard, his tunic: it is the man himself. I met him at the theater while Thaïs was displaying her skilful arms. He was greatly moved, and I can bear witness that he spake with vehemence. He is an honorable man: he will curse us; his eloquence is terrible. If Marcus is the Plato of the Christians, Paphnutius is the Demosthenes. Epicurus, in his little garden, never heard anything like it."

Philinna and Drosea, however, were devouring Thaïs with their eyes. She wore on her blonde hair a crown of pale violets, each flower of which revealed, in a feeble way, the color of her eyes, so much so, that the flowers seemed half-hidden glances and the eyes sparkling flowers. It was this woman's gift: on her everything lived, everything was soul and harmony. Her mauve robe, embroidered with silver wire, had in its long folds a grace almost sad and unrelieved by bracelets or necklace, and all the glory of her attire was in her neck and arms. While admiring, in spite of themselves, the robe and coiffure of Thaïs, her two friends did not speak to her of them.

"How beautiful you are," said Philinna. "You could not have been more beautiful when you came to Alexandria. But, my mother, who remembers seeing you then, said that few women were worthy of comparison with you."

"Who then," said Drosea, "is this new lover of yours? He has a wild appearance. If there were elephant keepers, surely they would be made like him. Where did you find, Thaïs, such a fierce friend? Was it not among the cave dwellers, who live under the earth and are tinged by the smoke of Hades?"

But Philinna, placing her finger upon Drosea's mouth, said:

"Be quiet, the mysteries of love remain secrets and their knowledge is forbidden. For myself, I would rather be kissed by the mouth of smoking Etna than by this man's lips. But our sweet Thaïs, who is as beautiful and adorable as a goddess, must, like a goddess, grant all prayers, and not, as we do, only those of lovable men."

"Take care, both of you," replied Thaïs. "He is a magician and enchanter. He understands words spoken in a low voice, and even thoughts. He will snatch your heart from you while you are asleep; he will replace it by a sponge, and on the morrow, after drinking water, you will die of suffocation."

"Friends, take your places! Slaves, pour out the honey-colored wine!"

Then the host, raising his cup, said:

"Drink first to the divine Constantius and the Empire's genius. The fatherland must be placed first, even before the gods, for it contains them."

All the guests raised their brimming cups to their lips. Paphnutius alone did not drink, because Constantius persecuted the faith of Nicaea, and the Christian's fatherland is not of this world.

Dorion, after drinking, murmured:

"What is the fatherland? A flowing river. Its banks change and waves are always upon it."

"I know, Dorion," replied the prefect of the fleet, "that you take little account of civic virtues, and that you think that the sage should live a stranger to business. I think, on the other hand, that an honorable man should desire nothing so much as to fill high offices in the State. What a beautiful thing the State is!"

Hermodorus, High Priest of Serapis, spoke:

"Dorion has just asked: 'What is the fatherland?' I will reply: The altars of the gods and the tombs of ancestors compose the fatherland. One man is another man's fellow citizen through a community of souvenirs and hopes."

Young Aristobulus interrupted Hermodorus:

"By Castor, I saw a fine horse to-day. It belongs to Demophon. It has a lean head and fine shoulders. It carries its head high and proud like a cock's."

But young Chereas shook his head.

"It is not as good a horse as you make out, Aristobulus. It has thin hoofs. Its pasterns are near the ground and the animal will soon go lame."

They were continuing their dispute, when Drosea uttered a piercing shriek.

"Oh! I almost swallowed a fish bone longer and sharper than a dagger. By good luck I drew it from my throat in time. The gods love me."

"Did you not say that the gods love you?" asked Nicias, with a smile. "If so, they share men's infirmity. Love supposes with the person who feels it the sentiment of eternal misery. It is by it that the weakness of beings is betrayed. The love which the gods feel for Drosea is a great proof of their imperfection."

At these words Drosea became very angry.

"Nicias, your words are silly and form no answer. Besides, it is your character not to understand what is said, and to reply in words utterly without sense."

Nicias smiled again.

"Speak, speak, Drosea. No matter what you say, we ought to return thanks every time you open your mouth. Your teeth are so beautiful."

At this moment a grave old man, negligently attired, entered the hall with a slow step and haughty bearing, and walked towards the guests. Cotta motioned to him to sit by his side, upon his own couch.

"Welcome, Eucritus," said he. "Have you written a new

treatise this month? It should be, if my calculation is correct, the ninety-second which has flowed from the Nile reed, which you guide with an Attic hand."

Eucritus replied as he caressed his silvery beard:

"The nightingale is made to sing and I am made to praise the immortal gods."

Dorion.—Let us respectfully salute in Eucritus the last of the Stoics. Grave and white, he rises in our midst like an ancestral image! He is alone in the crowd of men and pronounces words which are not understood.

Eucritus.—You are mistaken, Dorion. The philosophy of virtue is not dead in this world. I have numerous disciples in Alexandria, Rome, and Constantinople. Many among the slaves and nephews of the Cæsars still know how to govern themselves, to live free and taste in abstinence illimitable felicity. Several revive in themselves Epictetus and Marcus Aurelius. But if it were true that virtue was forever extinct upon the earth, in what way would its loss concern my happiness, since its duration or death does not depend on me? Only fools, Dorion, place their felicity beyond their own power. I desire nothing the gods do not will, and I desire all they will. By this means I become like them and partake of their infallible contentment. If virtue perish, I consent to its death and the consent fills me with joy like the supreme effort of my reason or my courage. In all things my wisdom will imitate divine wisdom, and the copy will be more precious than the model; it will have cost more care and labor.

Nicias.—I understand. You associate yourself with celestial Providence. But if virtue consists only in effort, Eucritus, and in that tension by which the disciples of Zeno pretended to render themselves like gods, the frog which swells out to become as large as the ox accomplishes the masterpiece of Stoicism.

Eucritus.—Nicias, you joke, and as usual excel in mockery.

But if the ox you speak of is really a god, as Apis and as the subterranean bull, whose High Priest I see here, and if the frog, wisely inspired, succeeds in equalling it, will it not be in reality more virtuous than the ox, and who will be able to stifle their admiration for so generous a little animal?

Four servants placed upon the table a wild pig still covered with bristles. Young boars, made of paste baked in an oven, surrounded the animal and indicated that it was a sow.

Zenothemis, turning towards the monk, said:

"Friend, a guest is come of himself to join us. The illustrious Paphnutius, who leads in solitude a wondrous life, is our unexpected guest."

Cotta.—Say more, Zenothemis. The first place is his due, since he has come uninvited.

Zenothemis.—We ought, too, dear Lucius, to receive him with particular kindness and find out what is most agreeable to him. Now it is certain that such a man is less sensible to the flavor of viands, than to the perfume of beautiful thoughts. We shall no doubt give him pleasure by directing the conversation upon the doctrine he professes, that of Jesus crucified. For myself, I shall lend myself the more willingly as that doctrine keenly interests me on account of the number and diversity of the allegories it includes. If the spirit beneath the letter is understood, it is full of truths, and I think the books of the Christians abound in divine revelations. But I could not set an equal value, Paphnutius, on the books of the Jews. They were inspired, not, as it has been said, by the spirit of God, but a bad spirit. Jehovah, who dictated them, was one of those spirits which people the lower air and cause the greater part of the ills we suffer; but he exceeds them all in ignorance and ferocity. On the other hand, the serpent with golden wings, which twisted round the tree of knowledge its azure coils, was formed of light and love. Thus the struggle between these two powers, one of light, the other of darkness, was inevitable. It commenred in the world's early days. God had hardly returned to rest, Adam and Eve, the first man and woman, were living naked and happy in the Garden of Eden when Jehovah formed, unfortunately for them, the intention of ruling them and all the generations Eve already bore in her magnificent womb. As he possessed neither compass nor lyre, and was alike ignorant of science, which commands, and art which persuades, he frightened these two poor children by various apparitions, capricious menaces and thunderclaps. Adam and Eve, feeling his shadow upon them, pressed close together and their love redoubled in fear. The serpent had pity on them and resolved to teach them wisdom, so that, possessing knowledge, they would be no longer abused by lies. This enterprise required rare prudence, and the weakness of the first human pair rendered it almost desperate. The well-intentioned demon, however, attempted it. Unknown to Jehovah, who pretended to see all, but whose sight in reality was not very clear, he approached the two creatures, and chained their eyes with the splendor of his breastplate and the glory of his wings. Then he interested their minds by forming before them with his body, exact figures, such as the circle, the ellipse, and the spiral, whose admirable qualities have been recognized since the days of the Greeks. Adam, better than Eve, meditated upon these figures. But when the serpent began to speak, and teach them the highest truths, those which do not demonstrate themselves, he recognized that Adam, fashioned from red earth, was of too dense a nature to perceive these subtle forms of knowledge, and that Eve, on the contrary, being tenderer and more sensible, could easily understand them. So he talked to her in her husband's absence, to initiate his first . . .

Dorion.—Allow me, Zenothemis, to stop you here. At first I recognized in the myth you are expounding to us, an episode in the struggle of Pallas Athenæ and the giants.

Jehovah very much resembles Typhon, and Pallas is represented by the Athenians with a serpent by her side. But what
you have just said has made me suddenly doubt the intelligence or good faith of the serpent of whom you speak. If he
had really possessed wisdom, would he have entrusted it to a
little woman's head incapable of containing it? I think that
he was, like Jehovah, ignorant and a liar, and that he chose
Eve because she was most easy to seduce, and because he gave
Adam credit for more intelligence and reflection.

Zenothemis.—Understand, Dorion, that it is not by reflection and intelligence, but by perception, that the highest and
purest truths are attained. Thus, women, who are usually
less reflective but more sensible than men, rise more easily to
knowledge of divine matters. In them is the gift of prophecy,
and it is not unreasonable for Apollo, Athenæ and Jesus of
Nazareth to be sometimes represented clothed as women in
long flowing robes. The serpent teacher was wise, whatever
you may say to the contrary, Dorion, in preferring for his
work of light this Eve, whiter than milk and the stars, to the
more gross and stupid Adam. She listened docilely and allowed herself to be led to the tree of knowledge, whose
branches stretched up to the sky, and upon which the Holy
Spirit rested like dew. This tree was covered with leaves,
which spake all the languages of future races, and whose
united voices formed perfect harmony. Its abundant fruits
gave to the initiated, who fed upon them, the knowledge of
metals, stones, plants, as well as of physical and moral laws;
but they were of flame, and those who feared suffering and
death dared not lift them to their lips. Now, after listening
to the serpent's teaching, Eve rose above vain terrors and
desired to taste the fruits, which gave knowledge of God.
But in order that Adam, whom she loved, might not become
her inferior, she took him by the hand and led him to the
marvelous tree. Plucking an apple of fire, she bit it, and
afterwards offered it to her companion. Unfortunately

Jehovah, who was walking by chance in the garden, surprised them, and seeing that they had become wise, he became terribly angry. He is specially to be feared when jealous. Collecting his forces, he produced such a tumult in the lower air that these two feeble beings were frightened at it. The fruit fell from the man's hand, and the woman, clinging to his neck, said: "I desire to be ignorant and suffer with you." Jehovah, in triumph, keeps Adam and Eve and all their seed in stupor and in fear. His art, which became reduced to fashioning great meteors, placed him beyond the power of the serpent's knowledge, though he was a musician and mathematician. He taught men injustice, ignorance, and cruelty, and caused evil to reign on earth. He pursued Cain and his sons because they were industrious; he exterminated the Philistines because they composed Orphic poems and fables like Æsop. He was the implacable enemy of knowledge and beauty, and mankind for long centuries expiated in tears and blood the defeat of the winged serpent. Fortunately learned men lived among the Greeks, such as Pythagoras and Plato, and they recovered by the power of genius the figures and ideas which Jehovah's enemy had vainly tried to teach the first woman. The spirit of the serpent was in them; for that reason, as Dorion says, the serpent is honored among the Athenians. Lastly, in later years, there appeared in human form three celestial spirits, Jesus of Galilee, Basilides, and Valentine, to whom it was given to pluck the finest fruits of the tree of knowledge, the roots of which traverse the earth and which rears its top to the heights of heaven. This is my revenge for the Christians, to whom the errors of the Jews are often imputed.

Dorion.—If I have understood you rightly, Zenothemis, three admirable men, Jesus, Basilides, and Valentine, have discovered secrets which were hidden to Pythagoras, Plato, all the philosophers of Greece, and even the divine Epicurus, who, however, freed men from all vain terror. You will oblige us by telling us by what means these three mortals acquired knowledge which escaped the meditation of the sages.

Zenothemis.—Must I repeat for your benefit, Dorion, that science and meditation are only the first degree of knowledge, and that ecstasy alone leads to eternal truths?

Hermodorus.—It is true, Zenothemis, that the soul is nourished on ecstasy, as the grasshopper is on dew. But let us go further: the spirit alone is capable of entire rapture. For man is triple, composed of a material body, a more subtle but equally material soul, and an incorruptible spirit. After leaving its body as a palace given up to silence and solitude, then flying across the gardens of its soul, the spirit is bestowed on God, it tastes the delights of an anticipated death, or rather of future life, for death is life, and in this state, which partakes of divine purity, it possesses at the same time infinite joy and absolute knowledge. It enters into unity, which is everything. It is perfect.

Nicias.—This is admirable. But to tell the truth, Hermodorus, I see no great difference between everything and nothing. Words even seem to fail me to make the distinction. The infinite resembles in a terrible degree nothingness: they are both inconceivable. In my opinion, perfection costs very dear: a person pays for it with his whole being, and to possess it one must cease to exist. That is a disgrace which God himself has not escaped, since philosophers have gone about to perfect him. After that, if we do not know what "not to be" is, we are also ignorant of what "to be" is. We know nothing. People say it is impossible for men to understand each other. I should think, in spite of our disputes, that, on the contrary, it is impossible for them not to finally agree, buried side by side under the masses of contradiction which they have heaped up, like Ossa upon Pelion.

Cotta.—I love philosophy very much, and I have studied it in my leisure hours. But I only understand it well in Cicero's works. Slaves, pour out the honey-colored wine!

Callicrates.—That is a singular thing! When I am sober, I think of the time when the tragic poets sat at the banquets of good tyrants, and my mouth waters. But when I have tasted the excellent wine you pour out for us, generous Lucius, I dream only of civil struggles and heroic combats. I blush to live in inglorious days, I invoke liberty, and in imagination shed my blood with the last of the Romans on the fields of Philippi.

Cotta.—At the decline of the Republic my kinsmen died with Brutus for liberty. But it is open to question whether, what they called the liberty of the Roman people, was not, in reality, the faculty of governing them themselves. I do not deny that liberty may be a nation's greatest good. But the longer I live, the more I persuade myself that a strong government alone can assure its citizens. I have filled for forty years the highest State office, and my long experience teaches me that people are oppressed when power is weak. So those who, as most rhetors do, try to weaken the government commit a detestable crime. If one man's will is sometimes used in a fatal manner, popular consent renders all resolution impossible. Before the majesty of Roman peace covered the world races were only happy under intelligent despots.

Hermodorus.—As for me, Lucius, I think there is no good form of government, and one will not be discovered, since the ingenious Greeks, who conceived so many happy forms, sought it in vain. In this direction every hope is henceforth forbidden us. We recognize by certain signs that the world is near sinking into ignorance and barbarity. It was given us, Lucius, to assist at the terrible agony of civilization. Of all the satisfaction which intelligence, science, and virtue procured, there only remains to us the cruel joy of watching ourselves die.

Cotta.—It is certain that the people's hunger and the

audacity of the barbarians are scourges to be feared. But, with a good fleet, a good army, and good finances . . .

Hermodorus.—What is the use of flattery? The expiring Empire offers the barbarians an easy prey. The cities, which were edified by Helenic genius and Latin patience, will soon be sacked by drunken savages. There will be on the earth no art or philosophy. The images of the gods will be overturned in the temples and in men's souls. It will be the night of the spirit and the death of the world. How, in fact, is it impossible to believe that the Sarmatians will ever undertake works of intelligence, that the Quadi and Marcomanni will adore the immortal gods. No; everything is tottering and sinking. This old Egypt, which has been the cradle of the world, will be its hypogee; Serapis, the god of death, will receive the supreme adoration of mortality, and I shall be the last priest of the last god.

At this moment a strange figure lifted the tapestry, and the guests saw before them a little hunchbacked man, whose bald head rose up to a point. He was dressed in the Asiatic fashion with an azure tunic, and wore upon his legs, like the barbarians, red breeches sewn with golden stars. When he saw him, Paphnutius recognized Marcus the Aryan, and, fearing a thunderbolt would fall, he raised his hands above his head and paled with fear. The mere presence of this heretic stunned his courage, a thing which, at the banquet of demons, neither the blasphemies of the Pagans nor the horrible errors of the philosophers had succeeded in doing. He wished to flee, but when his glance met the glance of Thaïs, he was suddenly reassured. He had read her soul and understood that she, who was about to become a saint, was already protecting him. He seized part of her flowing robe and mentally prayed to the Saviour Jesus.

A flattering murmur accompanied the arrival of the person, who was called the Plato of the Christians. Hermodorus spoke to him first:

"Most illustrious Marcus, we all rejoice to see you among

us, and your arrival is very opportune. We know of the
Christian doctrine only what is publicly taught. Now it is
certain that a philosopher like you cannot think with the
vulgar, and we are anxious to know your opinion of the
principal mysteries of the religion you profess. Our dear
Zenothemis, whom you know is very fond of symbols, was
just now asking Paphnutius about the books of the Jews.
But Paphnutius has not replied to him, and we must not be
surprised at this, since our guest is vowed to silence and God
has sealed his tongue in the desert. But you, Marcus, who
have spoken in the Christian synods, and even the councils of
the divine Constantine, you can, if you wish, satisfy our
curiosity by revealing to us the philosophic truths which are
hidden in the fables of the Christians. Is not the first of these
truths the existence of an only God, in whom I, for my part,
firmly believe?"

Marcus.—Yes, venerable brothers, I believe in an only
God, not begotten, the one eternal, the beginning of all
things.

Nicias.—We know, Marcus, that your God created the
world. It was indeed a great crisis in his existence. He was
existing for an eternity before being able to resolve to do so.
But, in justice, admit his situation was a very awkward one.
He had to remain inactive to remain perfect, and he had to
act if he desired to prove himself his own existence. You
assure me that he decided to act. I will believe you, Marcus,
although it is on the part of a perfect God an unpardonable
imprudence. But tell us, Marcus, how he set about creating
the world.

Marcus.—Those who, without being Christians, possess, as
Hermodorus and Zenothemis do, the principles of knowledge,
know that God did not create the world directly and without
intervention. He gave birth to an only son, by whom all
things were made.

Hermodorus.—You are right, Marcus; and this son is

adored under the names of Hermes, Mithra, Adonis, Apollo, and Jesus.

Marcus.—I should not be a Christian if I gave him names other than Jesus Christ and Saviour. He is the true son of God. But he is not eternal, since he had a beginning; as for thinking he existed before being begotten, that is an absurdity which must be left to the mules of Nicaea and the restive ass who too long ruled the church of Alexandria under the cursed name of Athanasius.

At these words, Paphnutius, who was pale, and whose forehead was bathed in the sweat of agony, made the sign of the Cross and persevered in his sublime silence.

Marcus continued:

"It is clear that the inept symbol of Nicaea makes an attempt on the majesty of the only God by obliging him to divide his indivisible attributes with its own emanation the mediator by whom all things were made. Cease to rail at the true God of the Christians, Nicias; learn that he works or spins no more than do the lilies of the field. He was not the workman; it was Jesus who created the world and afterwards came to repair his work. For the creation could not be perfect and evil was of necessity mixed with good in it."

Nicias.—What is good and what is evil?

There was a moment's silence, during which Hermodorus, with his arms stretched upon the table displayed a little donkey of Corinthian metal, carrying two baskets, one containing white olives and the other black.

"Look at these olives," said he. "Our looks are agreeably flattered by the contrast of their tints, and we are satisfied that these are clear and those dark. But if they were endowed with thought and knowledge, the white ones would say: 'It is well for an olive to be white, ill for it to be black,' and the people of the black olives would detest those of the white. We judge better, for we are as much above them as the gods are above us. For man, who sees only a part of everything, evil is a blessing. Without doubt, ugliness is ugly and not beautiful; but if everything was beautiful, everything would not be beautiful. It is then well for there to be evil greater than the first."

Eucritus.—Let us speak more virtuously. Evil is an evil, not to the world whose indestructible harmony it does not destroy, but to the sinner who commits it and could not do so.

Cotta.—By Jupiter! that is fine reasoning!

Eucritus.—The world is a tragedy by an excellent poet. God, who composed it, has designed each of us to play a part in it. If he desires you to be beggar, prince, or cripple, do your best with the part assigned you.

Nicias.—Assuredly it will be good for the cripple of the tragedy to limp like Hephaistos; it will be good for the madman to abandon himself to the furies of Ajax, for the incestuous woman to renew the crimes of Phaedra, for the traitor to betray, for the cheat to lie, for the murderer to kill, and, when the piece is played, all the actors, kings, the just, bloody tyrants, pious virgins, shameless wives, magnanimous citizens and cowardly assassins will receive from the poet an equal share of praise.

Eucritus.—You pervert my idea, Nicias, and change a lovely girl into a hideous gorgon. I feel sorry for your ignorance of the nature of the gods, justice, and eternal laws.

Zenothemis.—I myself, friends, believe in the reality of good and evil. But I am persuaded that it is not a single human action, were it even the kiss of Judas, which bears a germ of redemption. Evil cooperates in the final salvation of men, and in that it proceeds from the good, and participates in the merit attached to it. That is what the Christians have admirably expressed by the fable of the red-haired man who, to betray his master, gave him the kiss of peace, and assured by that act men's safety. So nothing, in my idea, is more unjust or vain than the hatred with which certain of the disciples of Paul pursue the most unfortunate of the apostles of Jesus, without thinking that the kiss of the Iscariot, prophesied by Jesus himself, was necessary, according to their own doctrine, for the redemption of men, and that, if Judas had not accepted the purse of thirty shekels, divine wisdom would have been belied, Providence deceived, its designs overthrown, and the world given over to evil, ignorance, and death.

Marcus.—Divine wisdom had foreseen that Judas, though at liberty not to give the traitor's kiss, would, nevertheless, give it. Thus it employed the Iscariot's crime as a stone in the marvelous edifice of redemption.

Zenothemis.—I spoke to you just now, Marcus, as if I believed that the redemption of men had been accomplished by the crucified Jesus, because I know that such is the Christian belief; and I entered into their thoughts the better to seize upon the failing of those who believe in the eternal damnation of Jesus. But in reality Jesus is, in my eyes, the harbinger of Basilides and Valentine. As to the mystery of the redemption, I will tell you, my dear friends, if you are at all curious to hear it, the way in which it was truly accomplished on earth.

The guests made signs of assent. Just at this moment twelve young girls, carrying on their heads baskets of pomegranates and apples, entered the hall with light steps, keeping time to an invisible flute, like the Athenian virgins with the sacred baskets of Ceres. They placed the baskets upon the table, the music of the flute ceased, and Zenothemis spoke as follows:—

"When Eunoia, the thought of God, had created the world, the government of the earth was entrusted to angels. They, however, did not preserve the calm proper to masters. Seeing that the daughters of men were beautiful, they surprised them in the evening on the banks of the water tanks, and were united to them. Of these hymens there was born a ferocious race, which covered the earth with injustice and cruelty, and the dust of the wayside drank up innocent blood. At this sight Eunoia was seized with infinite sadness.

" 'This is my doing,' she sighed, leaning towards the world. 'My poor children are plunged, through my fault, into a life of bitterness. Their suffering is my crime, and I desire to expiate it. God himself, who thinks only by me, would be powerless to return to them their primal purity. What is done is done, and the creation is forever spoiled. At least, I will not abandon my creatures. If I cannot make them as happy as myself, I can make myself as unhappy as they are. Since I have made the mistake of giving them bodies which humiliate them, I myself will assume a body like unto theirs, and go and live amongst them.'

"After saying this, Eunoia descended to earth, and became incarnate in the womb of an Argive woman. After birth she was weak and she received the name of Helen. She soon, however, grew in grace and beauty, and became the most greatly desired of women, as she had resolved to commit in her mortal body the most noble sins. The inner prey of lewd and violent men, she devoted herself to rape and adultery, in expiation of all adultery, violence, and iniquity, and caused by her beauty the ruin of races, in order that God might pardon the crimes of the universe. Never was the idea of heaven, never was Eunoia so adorable as in the days when, as a woman, she prostituted herself to heroes and shepherds. Poets divined her divinity, when they depicted her so peaceful, superb, and so fatal, and when they made this invocation to her: 'Soul serene as the calm upon the sea!'

"Thus was Eunoia dragged out of pity into evil and suffering. She died, and the Argive race still show her tomb, for she had to know death after pleasure, and taste all the bitter fruits she had sown. But, escaping from Helen's decomposing flesh, she became incarnate in another woman's form, and again submitted to every outrage. Thus, passing from body to body, and traversing the ages of evil among us, she takes upon her the sins of the world. Her sacrifice will not be vain. Attached to us by the bonds of the flesh, loving and weeping with us, she will work out her own and our redemption, and will delight us, suspended at her white breast, with the peace of a conquered heaven."

Hermodorus.—This myth is not unknown to me. I remember that it is said that, in one of her metamorphoses, this divine Helen lived with Simon the magician in the days of the Emperor Tiberius. Still, I thought that her downfall was involuntary, and that the angels had involved her in their own ruin.

Zenothemis.—Hermodorus, it is true that men ill informed in the mysteries have thought that sorrowing Eunoia had not agreed to her own destruction. But if it were as they pretend, Eunoia would not be the atoning courtesan, covered with all blemishes, the bread soaked in the wine of our shame, the meritorious sacrifice, the agreeable offering, the holocaust whose smoke mounts to God. Had not her sins been voluntary, they would have no virtue.

Callicrates.—But is it not known, Zenothemis, in what country, under what name, in what adorable form, this ever re-born Helen lives to-day?

Zenothemis.—A man must be very wise to discover such a secret. And wisdom, Callicrates, is not given to poets, who live in the vulgar world of forms and amuse themselves like children with sounds and vain images.

Callicrates.—Fear to offend the gods, impious Zenothemis, poets are dear to them. The first laws were dictated in verse by the immortals themselves, and the oracles of the gods are poems. Hymns are agreeable in sound to celestial ears. Who knows that poets are not seers, and nothing is hidden from them. Being a poet myself, and crowned with the laurels of Apollo, I will reveal to all the last incarnation of Eunoia. Eternal Helen is near you; she looks at us, and we look at her.

Do you see that woman reclining on the cushions of her couch, so beautiful and so thoughtful, in whose eyes are tears, and on whose lips kisses. It is she! charming as in the days of Priam, and Asia's glory, to-day Eunoia is called Thaïs.

Philinna.—What is that you are saying, Callicrates? Our dear Thaïs would have known Paris, Menelaus, and the Achæans who fought before Ilium! Was the horse of Troy large, Thaïs?

Aristobulus.—Who speaks of a horse?

"I have drunk like a Thracian!" cried Chereas, as he rolled under the table.

Callicrates, raising his cup, said:

"If we drink desperately, we shall die without vengeance!"

Old Cotta slept, his bald head balanced upon his broad shoulders.

For some time Dorion seemed much disturbed under his cloak of philosophy. He approached the couch of Thaïs murmuring:

"Thaïs, I love you, although it is unworthy of me to love a woman."

Thaïs.—Why did you not love me before?

Dorion.—Because I was fasting.

Thaïs.—I, poor friend, who have drunk only water, permit me not to love you.

Dorion did not desire to hear more, and glided towards Drosea, who ordered him with a look to raise his friend. Zenothemis took the vacant place, and kissed Thaïs on the lips.

Thaïs.—I thought you were more virtuous.

Zenothemis.—I am perfect, and the perfect are bound by no law.

Thaïs.—But do you not fear to soil your soul in a woman's arms?

Zenothemis.—The body can yield to desire without the soul being affected.

Thaïs.—Go away! I want to be loved both body and soul. All these philosophers are goats!

One by one the lamps went out. Pale dawn, penetrating through the openings of the tapestry, lit up the livid faces and swollen eyes of the guests. Aristobulus, who had fallen by the side of Chereas with clenched hands, was sending in his dream his grooms to the ravens. Zenothemis was pressing in his arms pale Philinna. Dorion was pouring upon Drosea's bare throat drops of wine, which rolled like rubies down her white breast heaving with laughter, pursued by the philosopher's lips to drink them from her flesh. Eucritus rose, and placing his arms upon the shoulders of Nicias, he led him to the back of the hall.

"Friend," he said, with a smile, "if you are still thinking, of what are you thinking?"

"I am thinking that women's loves are the gardens of Adonis."

"What do you mean?"

"Don't you know, Eucritus, that women construct every year little gardens upon their terraces by planting palms for the lover of Venus in vases of clay. These palms are green for a short time and then fade."

"What does it matter, Nicias? It is folly to attach oneself to that which passes away."

"If beauty is only a shadow, desire is only a beam. What folly it is to desire beauty! Is it not reasonable, on the other hand, for that which passes away to go to that which does not endure, and for the light to devour the disappearing shadow?"

"Nicias, you seem to me like a child playing at hucklebones. Believe me; be free. That is how to become a man."

"How can a person be free, Eucritus, when he has a body?"

"You shall see at once, my son. In a moment you will say: Eucritus was free." The old man, as he spoke, was leaning upon a porphyry column, his forehead lit up by the first rays of dawn. Hermodorus and Marcus, having approached, stood before him by the side of Nicias, and all four, indifferent to the laughter and cries of the drinkers, talked of divine matters. Eucritus expressed himself so wisely that Marcus said to him:

"You are worthy to know the true God."

Eucritus replied:

"The true God is in the wise man's heart."

Then they spoke of death.

"I desire it," said Eucritus, "to find me occupied in self-correction and attentive to all my duties. Before it I will raise my pure hands to heaven and say to the gods: 'Your images, O gods, which you have placed in the temple of my soul, I have not soiled. I have hung my thoughts there like garlands, bands, and crowns. I have lived in conformity to your providence. I have lived enough.' "

Speaking thus, he raised his arms to heaven and his face shone with light.

He remained pensive for a moment. Then he resumed, with cheerfulness:

"Detach yourself from life, Eucritus, like the ripe olive which falls, returning thanks to the tree that bore it, and blessing the earth, its nurse!"

At these words, drawing from the folds of his robe a naked dagger, he plunged it into his breast.

When his listeners seized his hand, the point of the dagger had pierced the wise man's heart. Eucritus had entered into rest. Hermodorus and Nicias bore the pale bleeding body to one of the couches, amid the piercing shrieks of the women, the groans of the guests disturbed from their sleep, and the stifled sighs of pleasure from the shadow of the hangings. Old Cotta, who had awakened from his light sleep with a soldier's promptitude, was already by the side of the corpse examining the wound, and exclaiming:

"Call my doctor, Aristeus!"

Nicias shook his head:

"Eucritus is no more," said he. "He desired death as others desire love. He has, like all of us, obeyed ineffable desire. Now he is as the gods who desire nothing."

Cotta beat his brow:

"Death, desire death, when a man can still serve the State, what rubbish!"

Paphnutius and Thaïs had remained motionless side by side, their souls overflowing with disgust, horror, and hope.

Suddenly the monk seized the actress by the hand, stepped with her over drunken men lying upon the floor, avoided men and women in each other's embrace, and dragged her out through the wine and blood.

Day was breaking on the city. Long colonnades stretched out on either side of the deserted road, which was topped in the distance by the gleaming pinnacle of Alexander's tomb. Upon the pathway were scattered here and there leafless crowns and extinct torches. In the air was the fresh breath of the sea. Paphnutius snatched off in disgust his sumptuous robe and trampled the shreds of it beneath his feet.

"You heard them, Thaïs," he cried. "They spoke of every folly and every abomination. They dragged the divine Creator of all things to the Gemoniae of the demons of hell, shamelessly denied good and evil, blasphemed Jesus, and boasted of Judas. And the most infamous of all, the jackals of the darkness, the stinking beast, the Aryan full of corruption and death, opened his mouth like a sepulcher. My Thaïs, you saw them creep towards you, those unclean slugs, and soil you with their slimy sweat; you saw those brutes sleeping beneath the slaves' feet; you saw those beasts coupled on the floor soiled by their own vomiting? You saw that mad old man spill blood more vile than the wine spilled in the debauch, and throw himself after the orgy into the face of the Christ unexpected by him! Praise be to God! You have looked upon error and seen that it was hideous. Thaïs, Thaïs, Thaïs, recall the folly of the philosophers, and say whether you wish to rave with them. Recall the looks, gestures, and laughter of their worthy comrades, those lascivious and malicious she apes, and say whether you desire to remain like them!"

Thaïs, whose heart had revolted at the disgust of that night, feeling the indifference and brutality of men, the wickedness of women, and the weight of the hours, sighed:

"I am wearied to death, my father! Where can rest be found? I feel my forehead burning, my head light, and my arms so weary, that I should not have strength to seize happiness if it were placed in my hands."

Paphnutius looked at her kindly:

"Courage, my sister," he said, "the hour of rest is approaching for you, who will become white and pure as the vapors which you can see oozing from those lakes and gardens."

They approached the house of Thaïs, and could see above the wall the heads of the plane trees and turpentine trees, which surrounded the Nymphs' grotto, quivering in the dew at the breath of the morning. A deserted square was before them, surrounded by columns and white statues, and having at its extremities semicircular marble benches, supporting chimeras. Thaïs dropped upon one of these benches. Then, casting an anxious glance at the monk, she asked: "What must I do?"

"You must," replied the monk, "follow him who has come to seek you. He is separating you from the world as the vintager gathers the bunch of grapes, which would rot upon the vine, and takes it to the wine press to turn it into perfumed wine. Listen: there is, twelve hours' journey from Alexandria towards the Occident, and near the sea, a nunnery, the regulations of which are masterpieces of wisdom, and deserve to be written in lyric verse and sung with an accompaniment of theorbos and tambourines. It can be truly said of the women who obey them that, with their feet on earth, they have their faces in heaven. In this world they live the lives of angels. They desire to be poor for Jesus to love them, modest for him to look at them, and chaste for him to espouse them. He visits them each day, dressed as a gardener, with naked feet and open hands—indeed, just as he showed himself to Mary on her way from the tomb. To-day I will take you to this nunnery, Thaïs, and soon after joining these holy women, you shall partake of their holy conversation. They are waiting for you like sisters. At the convent door their mother, pious Albina, will give you the kiss of peace, and say: 'Daughter, welcome!' "

The courtesan uttered an exclamation of admiration.

"Albina, a daughter of the Cæsars! The grandniece of the Emperor Carus!"

"Herself! Albina! who, born in the purple, reclad herself with sackcloth and, daughter of the masters of the world, rose to the rank of servant of Jesus Christ."

Thaïs got up and said: "Take me to Albina's house."

Paphnutius, to complete his victory, said: "I will indeed take you there; and enclose you in a cell, in which you shall weep for your sins; for it is not right for you to mix with Albina's daughters before being washed from all your stains. I will seal the door, and you shall wait, a happy prisoner, till Jesus himself comes, and as a sign of pardon breaks my seal. Do you doubt that he will come, Thaïs, and what a tremor will run through your flesh when you feel the fingers of light placed upon your eyes to dry your tears!"

Thaïs said for the second time: "Take me, father, to Albina's house."

With his heart full of joy, Paphnutius looked round him, and tasted, almost without fear, the pleasure of contemplating created things; his eyes drank in the light of God with delight, and unknown breaths passed across his forehead. Suddenly, recognizing in one of the angles of the square the small door leading to the house of Thaïs, and remembering that these fine trees, whose tops he was admiring, shaded the courtesan's garden, he saw in thought the impurities which had there soiled the air to-day so fresh and pure, and his soul was so grieved that a flood of bitter tears poured from his eyes.

"Thaïs," said he, "we will flee without turning our heads. But we will not leave behind us the instruments, the witnesses, the accomplices of your past crimes, those thick hangings, those beds, that tapestry, those urns of perfume, and those lamps which would proclaim your infamy. Do you desire this furniture of crime, animated by demons, and carried away by the cursed spirit that is in it, to follow you to the desert? It is only too true, that tables of scandal and seats of infamy serve as instruments for devils, acting, speaking, striking the earth and traversing the air. Let everything which partook of your shame perish! Hasten, Thaïs, and while the city is still asleep, order your slaves to build in the middle of this square a wood pile, upon which we will burn all the abominable wealth your dwelling contains."

Thaïs consented to this.

"Do as you like, my father," said she. "I know that sometimes inanimate objects serve as places of sojourn of spirits. At night, certain pieces of furniture speak, either by striking blows at regular intervals, or by showing little lights like signals. But still that is nothing. Did you not see, father, when entering the Nymphs' grotto, on the right, a statue of a naked woman about to bathe? One day I saw the statue turn its head, like a living person, and immediately resume its ordinary attitude. I was frozen with fear. Nicias, to whom I told this marvel, laughed at me; there is, however, some magic in the statue, for it inspired violent desire in a man named Dalnatius, who was insensible to my beauty. It is certain that I have been among enchantments, and have been exposed to the greatest dangers, for men have been stifled by the embrace of a brazen statue. It is, however, a pity to destroy precious things, made with rare industry, and if my tapestry and hangings are burned the loss will be great. The beauty of color in some of them is really admirable, and they cost the persons who gave them to me a great sum. I possess cups, statues, and pictures, the value of which is very great. I do not believe that it is necessary to destroy them. But you, father, knowing as you do what is necessary, do as you will."

Saying this, she followed the monk to the little door, where so many crowns and garlands had been hung, and opening it, ordered the porter to call all the slaves in the house. Four Indian cooks appeared; they were yellow-skinned, and all blind of one eye. Thaïs had had great trouble and much amusement in collecting four slaves of the same race, afflicted by the same disease. When they served at table, they excited the curiosity of the guests, and Thaïs made them tell the story of their lives. They approached in silence. Their assistants followed them. Then came the grooms, the huntsmen, the litter bearers, and the tireless couriers, two gardeners, hairy as Priapus, six negroes of ferocious appearance, and three Greek slaves, one a grammarian, another a poet, and the third a singer. They were all ranged in order in the square, when the curious negresses arrived in haste, uneasily rolling their large eyes and extending their mouths as far as their earrings. Last of all, adjusting their veils, and languidly moving their feet, which were fettered with thin gold chains, appeared six beautiful white slaves, looking very disagreeable. When they were all together, Thaïs said, as she pointed out Paphnutius to them:

"Do as this man orders you, for the spirit of God is in him, and if you disobey him, you will fall dead."

She believed this, for she had heard that the holy men of the desert had the power to plunge the wicked, who struck them with their rods, into the open and smoking earth.

Paphnutius sent away the women and the Greek slaves, who were like women, and said to the others:

"Bring wood into the middle of the square, make a great fire, and throw upon it all the contents of the house and grotto."

They stood motionless with surprise, and interrogated their mistress with their eyes. As she remained inert and silent, they crowded together in a heap, shoulder to shoulder, uncertain if it were a joke or not.

"Obey," said the monk.

Several were Christians. Understanding the order given them, they went into the house to find wood and torches. The others followed their example without feeling displeased, for, being poor, they hated wealth, and instinctively had a taste for destruction. As they built the pile of wood, Paphnutius said to Thaïs:

"I thought for a moment of calling the treasurer of some Alexandrian church (if there is one worthy of the name of church, and unsoiled by Aryan beasts), and giving him your property, woman, to distribute to widows, and thus change the gain of crime into the treasury of justice. But this thought did not come from God, so I repulsed it, and to offer the well beloved of Christ the spoils of luxury would be a grave offense. Thaïs, everything you have touched must be devoured by fire to the uttermost. Thanks be to heaven these tunics and veils, which have received kisses as countless as the waves of the sea, will now feel but lips and tongues of flame. Slaves, hasten! Bring more wood and torches! Woman, enter the house, take off your infamous garments, and beg of the humblest of your slaves, as a great favor, her oldest tunic."

Thaïs obeyed. While kneeling Indians blew upon the burning brands, negroes threw upon the pile coffers of ivory, ebony, or cedar, which, opening, threw out crowns, garlands, and necklaces. The smoke rose in a dark column, like the acceptable sacrifices of the ancient law. Then the smoldering fire suddenly burst out, roared like a monster beast, and with almost invisible flames began to devour its precious fuel.

Then the slaves grew bold at their work; they quickly dragged out rich tapestry, veils embroidered in silver, and flowered hangings. They bent beneath the weight of tables, couches, thick cushions, and beds with golden pins. Three strong Ethiopians ran, carrying in their arms the colored statues of the nymphs—one of which had been loved as a mortal—and they seemed like great apes carrying off women. When the beautiful naked forms fell from their arms, and broke upon the stones, a groan was heard.

At this moment Thaïs appeared, with her unbound hair hanging in long strands, her feet bare, and clad in a coarse and shapeless tunic, which, from simply touching her body, became impregnated with divine voluptuousness. Behind her came a gardener, bearing, hidden in his flowing beard, an ivory Eros.

She signed the man to stop, and, approaching Paphnutius, showed him the little god.

"Father," she asked, "must this, too, be thrown into the flames? It is of old and wonderful workmanship, and is worth a hundred times its weight in gold. Its loss will be irreparable, for there is no artist in the world capable of making another Eros so beautiful. Consider also, father, that this little child is Love, and he must not be beaten cruelly. Believe me, Love is a virtue, and if I have sinned it is not by him, father, but against him. Never shall I regret what he has made me do, and I weep only for what I have done in spite of his prohibition. He does not allow women to give themselves to those who do not come in his name. For that he should be honored. See, Paphnutius, how pretty this little Eros is! How gracefully he hides in the gardener's beard! One day Nicias, who loved me then, brought it to me, saying: 'It will speak to you of me.' But the naughty child spoke to me of a young man I had known at Antioch, and not of Nicias. Enough wealth has perished on this pile, father! Keep this Eros, and place it in some monastery. Those who see it

will turn their hearts to God, for Love knows by nature how
to rise to thoughts of heaven."

The gardener, thinking that the Eros was saved, was smiling upon it as upon a child, when Paphnutius, snatching the
god from the arms that held it, hurled it into the flames,
shouting:

"The fact of Nicias having touched it is sufficient to make
it spread every poison."

Then seizing handfuls of sparkling robes, purple mantles,
golden sandals, combs, mirrors, lamps, theorbos and lyres,
he threw them into the brazier, which was more sumptuous
than the funeral pile of Sardanapalus, while the slaves, drunk
with the joy of destruction, danced and shouted beneath a
hail of sparks and cinders.

One by one the neighbors, wakened by the noise, opened
their windows, and, rubbing their eyes, looked for the origin
of the smoke. Then they descended, half dressed, to the
square, and approached the pile: "What is that?" they
thought.

Among them were merchants from whom Thaïs used to
buy perfumes or stuffs, and these uneasily craned their yellow
withered heads in an effort to understand. Young profligates,
passing by on the way home from supper, preceded by their
slaves, stopped with flowers around their heads, and loosened
tunics, and uttered loud cries. The ever increasing crowd of
the curious soon knew that Thaïs, at the inspiration of the
priest of Antinoë, was burning her wealth before retiring to
a nunnery.

The merchants thought:

"Thaïs is leaving the city; we shall sell her nothing more;
that is frightful to contemplate. What will become of us
without her? This monk has made her lose her reason. He is
ruining us. Why is he allowed to do it? Of what use are
the laws? Are there no magistrates in Alexandria? Thaïs has
neither thought of our wives nor our poor children. Her con-

duct is a public scandal. She must be made to remain, in spite of herself, in the city."

The young men, on their side, thought:

"If Thaïs renounces the games, and love, our dearest amusements are gone. She was the delicious glory and superb honor of the theater. She was the joy of those who did not possess her. Women, whom a man loved, were loved in her; no kisses were exchanged from which her influence was quite absent, for she was the pleasure of pleasures, and the mere thought that she breathed among us excited us to pleasure."

So thought the young men, and one of them named Cerons, who had held her in his arms, cried out at the rape and blasphemed Christ. In every group the conduct of Thaïs was severely condemned.

"It's a shameful flight."

"A cowardly departure!"

"She is taking the bread from our mouths."

"She is taking away the dowries of our daughters."

"She will, at least, have to pay for the crowns I have sold her."

"And the sixty robes she has ordered from me."

"She is in debt to everyone."

"Who will take the parts of Iphigenia, Electra, and Polyxena after her? Beautiful Polybius will not succeed as she has done."

"Life will be a sad thing when her door is shut."

"She was the bright star, the soft moon in the Alexandrian sky."

The most celebrated beggars of the city, the blind, cripples, and paralytics had now assembled in the square; and, dragging themselves into the shadow of the riches, they groaned:

"How shall we live when Thaïs is not here to feed us? The meat from her table every day satisfied two hundred of the unfortunate, and her well-pleased lovers, on leaving her, used to throw us, as they passed, handfuls of silver."

Thieves in the crowd uttered deafening shouts, and hustled their neighbors to augment the disorder and profit by it by carrying off some valuable booty.

Old Thaddeus, who sold wool from Miletus, and flax from Tarentum, and to whom Thaïs owed a large sum of money, alone remained calm and silent in the midst of the tumult. Looking straight before him, and straining his ears, he caressed his goat's beard and seemed pensive. At last, approaching young Cerons, he plucked him by the sleeve and said to him in a low voice:

"You, my lord, whom Thaïs prefers, show yourself, and do not suffer her to be carried off by this monk."

"By Pollux and his sister, he shall not do it!" cried Cerons. "I will speak to Thaïs, and without flattering myself, I think she will hear me rather than this Lapithus daubed with soot. Make way, ruffians!"

After striking men with his fist, knocking down old women, and trampling on little children, he reached Thaïs, and drawing her aside:

"Lovely girl," said he, "look at me, recollect yourself, and tell me whether you really renounce love."

But Paphnutius, throwing himself between Thaïs and Cerons, cried:

"Wretch, prepare for death if you touch her; she is sacred, she belongs to God."

"Go away, dog-headed monk," replied the young man in a rage; "let me speak to my friend, or, if not, I will drag your obscene carcass by the beard to the fire and grill you alive upon it."

He stretched out his hand towards Thaïs. But, repulsed by the monk with unexpected violence, he staggered and fell four paces away at the foot of the pile among the falling brands.

Old Thaddeus, however, went from one to the other, pulling the slaves' ears, and kissing the masters' hands, exciting all of them against Paphnutius, and he soon formed a little band which marched resolutely at the ravisher monk. Cerons rose, with blackened face, singed hair, and almost suffocated with smoke and rage. He blasphemed the gods, and rushed on among the assailants, behind whom the beggars crawled, waving their crutches. Paphnutius was soon enclosed in a circle of outstretched hands, uplifted sticks, and death shouts.

"To the ravens with the monk!"

"No, throw him on the fire! Roast him alive!"

Seizing his beautiful prey, he pressed her to his heart.

"Wretches," he cried in a voice of thunder, "do not attempt to snatch away the dove from the eagle of the Lord. Rather imitate this woman, and, like her, change your mud to gold. Renounce, following her example, the false gods, your possessions, in which you believe. Hasten, the days are near, and divine patience begins to weary. Repent, confess your shame, weep and pray. Walk in the footsteps of Thaïs. Detest your crimes, which are as great as hers. Which of you, poor or rich, merchants, soldiers, slaves, or illustrious citizens, would dare to say before God that you were better than a courtesan? You are all uncleanness personified, and it is the miracle of heavenly goodness, that mud does not flow from you in streams."

While he spoke, flames flashed from his eyes; it seemed as if burning coals fell from his lips, and those about listened against their will.

But old Thaddeus did not remain idle. He was collecting stones and oyster shells, which he concealed in a fold of his tunic, and, not daring to throw them himself, he slid them into the hands of the beggars. Soon the stones flew, and a well-aimed shell struck the forehead of Paphnutius. The blood which flowed down the somber martyr's face, dropped as a new baptism upon the penitent's head, and Thaïs, oppressed by the monk's embrace, and her delicate flesh scratched by his rough robe, felt tremors of horror and fear surge through her limbs.

At this moment an elegantly dressed man, crowned with small-age, opened a path for himself to the middle of the surging mob, and cried:

"Stop, stop! This monk is my brother!" It was Nicias, who, after closing the eyes of the philosopher Eucritus, was passing through the square on the way to his house, and had seen, without very much surprise (for nothing ever astonished him), the smoking pile, Thaïs clad in sackcloth, and the stoning of Paphnutius.

He repeated:

"Stop, I tell you; spare my fellow pupil; respect the dear head of Paphnutius."

But, being accustomed to the subtle discourses of sages, he had not that imperious energy which overawes the minds of the people. They did not listen to him. A shower of pebbles and shells fell upon the monk who, covering Thaïs with his body, praised God whose goodness changed his wounds into caresses. Despairing of making himself heard, and well assured of his inability to save his friend, either by force or persuasion, Nicias had already designed his safety to the gods, in whom he had little confidence, when it came into his head to try a stratagem, which his contempt for men had suddenly suggested to him. He took from his girdle his purse which, as he was a man of pleasure and charitable, was full of gold and silver; then he ran to all those who were throwing stones and jingled the coins in their ears. At first they took no notice, so great was their fury; but little by little their eyes turned towards the jingling gold, and soon their enervated arms ceased to menace their victim. Seeing he had attracted their eyes and attention, Nicias opened his purse and began to throw among the crowd gold and silver coins. The most greedy stooped down to pick them up. The philoso-

pher, happy at his early success, cleverly threw the drachmæ
and deniers here and there. At the sound of the pieces of
metal bounding on the stones, the troop of persecutors went
to earth. Beggars, slaves, and merchants wallowed in com-
petition, while, grouped around Cerons, the patricians roared
with laughter as they looked at the sight. Cerons himself for-
got his anger. His friends encouraged the prostrate rivals,
chose champions, made bets upon them, and, when disputes
arose, urged on the wretches, as if they were fighting dogs.
When a cripple succeeded in seizing a drachma the shouting
was loud. The young men, too, began to throw coins, and
the only thing to be seen in the square was an infinity of
backs which, beneath a rain of metal, beat together like the
waves of a rough sea. Paphnutius was forgotten.

Nicias ran to him, covered him with his cloak, and
dragged him and Thaïs into lanes, where they would not be
pursued. They ran for a time in silence, then, judging themselves out of reach, they slackened their pace, and Nicias said,
a little sadly, in a mocking tone:

"Then it is done! Pluto ravished Proserpine, and Thaïs
desires to follow my fierce friend far from us."

"True, Nicias," Thaïs replied, "I am tired of living with
men like you, smiling, perfumed and kindly egoists. I am
weary of all I know, and I am seeking the unknown. I
learned by experience that joy was not true joy, and this man
teaches me that grief is the true joy. I believe him, for he
possesses the truth."

"I, beloved friend," Nicias replied, with a smile, "possess
the truths. He has only one of them; I have them all. I am
richer than he is, and, to tell the truth, neither prouder nor
happier."

Seeing the monk casting furious glances at him, he said:

"Dear Paphnutius, do not think that I consider you extremely ridiculous, or even quite unreasonable. If I compare
my life with yours, I should be able to say which was the

more preferable in itself. I am now going to have the bath Crobyle and Myrtale have prepared for me; I shall eat the wing of a pheasant from the Phasis, then I shall read for the hundredth time some fable from Apuleius, or some treatise by Porphyrius. You will return to your hut, where, kneeling like a docile camel, you will ruminate on some formulæ of incantation, which you have digested many times before, and in the evening you will eat radishes without oil. Ah, well, dear friend, in doing these things, which are totally different in appearance, we shall both obey the same sentiment, the sole motive of all human actions; we shall both of us be seeking our pleasure and be placing before ourselves a common end: happiness, impossible happiness! It would therefore be unkind of me to make you out to be wrong, dear friend, if I myself believe I am right.

"Thaïs, go and rejoice, be happier still, if that is possible, in abstinence and austerity than you have been in wealth and pleasure. Taking everything into consideration, I think you are to be envied. For if in our whole existence, obeying our nature, Paphnutius and I have pursued only one kind of satisfaction, you will have tasted in life, dear Thaïs, such opposite pleasures as are rarely given to one person to enjoy. In truth, I would like to be for an hour a holy man of the kind our friend Paphnutius is. But that is not permitted me. Adieu then, Thaïs! Go whither the secret powers of your nature and destiny lead you. Go, and take with you the good wishes of Nicias. I know the inanity of it; but can I give you anything better than sterile regrets and vain desires as the price of the delicious illusions which formerly enveloped me in your arms, the shadows of which still remain. Adieu, my benefactress! adieu, goodness, which ignores itself, mysterious virtue, men's pleasure! Adieu, the most adorable image nature has ever hurled to an unknown end upon the face of this deceitful earth!"

While he was speaking, anger was rising in the monk's heart; it showed itself in imprecations.

"Go away, wretch! I despise and hate you! Go away, child of hell, a thousand times worse than those poor sinners, who were just now hurling abuse and stones at me. They knew not what they did; and the grace of God, which I implore for them, may one day descend into their hearts. But you, hateful Nicias, are only perfidious venom and rank poison. The breath of your mouth exhales despair and death. One smile of yours contains more blasphemies than the smoking lips of Satan utter in a century!"

Nicias looked at him tenderly.

"Adieu, brother," he said to him, "may you keep till the final dissolution the treasures of your faith—hate and love! Adieu, Thaïs! It will be vain for you to forget me, since I am keeping you in remembrance."

Leaving them, he went thoughtfully through the tortuous streets near the great necropolis of Alexandria, in which the funeral potters dwelt. Their shops were full of clay figures, painted bright colors, representing gods and goddesses, pantomimes, women, and little winged genii, which were usually buried with the dead. He thought that perhaps some of the images at which he was looking would be the companions of his eternal sleep; and it seemed to him that a little Eros, with tucked-up tunic, was laughing a mocking laugh. The idea of his obsequies, which he pictured to himself, was painful to him. To relieve his sadness, he tried philosophy, and constructed a reason:

"Now," said he, "in truth, time has no reality. It is purely an illusion of our minds. Now, how can it, if it does not exist, bring me death? Is that saying I shall live forever? No; but by that I conclude that my death is, and always was, as much as it will be. I do not feel it yet, but still it exists, and I must not fear it, for it would be folly to fear the advent of that which has arrived. It exists like the last page of a book which I have read and not finished."

This reasoning occupied his walk without cheering him; he had a heavy heart when, as he reached his door, he heard the clear laughter of Crobyle and Myrtale, who were playing tennis while waiting for him.

Paphnutius and Thaïs left the city by the gate of the Moon, and walked along the seashore.

"Woman," said the monk, "the whole of this great blue sea could not wash away your stains."

He spoke to her in anger and contempt.

"Uncleaner than the dogs and swine, you have prostituted to the Pagans and unfaithful a body which the Eternal had formed for a tabernacle, and your impurities are such that, now you know the truth, you can no more close your lips or clasp your hands without disgust of yourself rising in your heart."

She followed him gently along rough roads, under a burning sun. Fatigue bent her knees, and thirst inflamed her breath. But, far from feeling that false pity which softens the hearts of the profane, Paphnutius rejoiced at the expiatory sufferings of this sinful flesh. In the transports of holy zeal, he would have liked to cut with rods this body, which retained its beauty as a striking testimony of its infamy. His meditations supported his pious fervor, and, recalling to his mind the fact that Thaïs had received Nicias into her bed, his horror of this sin became so great, that all his blood flowed back to his heart, and his breast was ready to burst. His curses, stifled in his throat, gave place to the grinding of his teeth. He sprang up, and stood before her, pale, terrible, full of God, looked down into her soul, and spat in her face.

She quietly wiped her face without halting. Then he followed her, looking down upon her as if she were an abyss. He walked in holy irritation. He thought of avenging Christ, so that Christ could not avenge himself, when he saw a spot

of blood which had dropped upon the sand from the foot of
Thaïs. Then he felt the freshness of an unknown breath enter
his open heart, sobs mounted to his lips in abundance, he
wept, he ran to prostrate himself before her, he called her his
sister, and kissed her bleeding feet. He murmured a hundred
times:

"My sister, my sister, my mother, most holy!"

He prayed:

"Angels of heaven, take this precious drop of blood, and
bear it to the Saviour's throne. May a miracle-working anem-
one flower in the sand watered by the blood of Thaïs, so
that all those who see this flower may recover purity of heart
and mind! O holy, holy, most holy Thaïs!"

As he prayed and prophesied, a boy rode by upon a donkey.
Paphnutius ordered him to dismount, seated Thaïs upon the
animal, took the bridle, and resumed the journey. Towards
evening, coming upon a canal shaded with beautiful trees, he
fastened the donkey to a tree, and, seating himself upon a
mossy stone, broke bread with Thaïs, and they ate it sea-
soned with salt and hyssop. They drank fresh water from
the palms of their hands, and conversed of things eternal. She
said:

"I have never drunk such pure water, nor breathed such
light air, and I feel that God floats in the passing breeze."

Paphnutius replied:

"See, it is evening, my sister. The blue shadows of the
night cover the hills. But you will soon see shining in the
dawn the tabernacle of life; you will soon see the rosy dawn
of the eternal morning."

They walked all night and, while the crescent moon lit up
the silver crests of the waves, sang psalms and canticles.
When the sun rose, the desert stretched before them like an
immense lion's skin spread upon Lybian soil. On the outskirts of the sand white huts stood out in the light of the
dawn, near some palm trees.

"Father," asked Thaïs, "are those the tabernacles of life?"

"You have said it, my daughter and sister," Paphnutius replied. "That is the house of refuge, in which I shall enclose you with my own hands."

Soon they could see on all sides women bestirring themselves around the Asiatic dwellings like bees around their hives. Some were baking bread, while others were preparing vegetables; several were spinning wool, and the light of heaven descended upon them like a smile from God. Others were meditating in the shade of the tamarisks; their white hands hung at their sides, for, being full of love, they had chosen the part of Magdalen, and they performed no duties except prayer and contemplation and ecstasy. For that reason they were called Marys, and were clothed in white. Those who worked with their hands were called Marthas, and wore blue robes. All were veiled, but the youngest allowed curls to hang down upon their foreheads, although it is possible that they did so unwittingly, as this was contrary to the rules. An extremely old lady, tall and white, was going from hut to hut, leaning upon a hard wood crutch, and Paphnutius approached her respectfully, kissed the edge of her veil, and said:

"The peace of God be with you, venerable Albina! I have brought to the hive, of which you are queen, a bee which I found lost upon a flowerless path. I have taken her in the hollow of my hand and warmed her with my breath. I give her to you."

He pointed with his fingers to the actress, who was kneeling before the daughter of the Cæsars.

Albina fixed a piercing glance upon Thaïs for a moment, ordered her to rise, kissed her forehead, and then, turning to the monk, she said:

"We will place her among the Marys."

Paphnutius then told her by what means Thaïs had been brought to the house of refuge, and asked for her to be first confined alone in a hut. The abbess consented; and led her to a hut left empty by the death of the virgin Laeta, who had sanctified it. There was in the narrow room only a bed, table and a pitcher, and Thaïs, when she put her foot upon the threshold, was filled with infinite joy.

"I desire to close her door myself," said Paphnutius, "and place a seal on it which Jesus will come and break."

He went to the edge of the fountain, took a handful of damp clay, put one of his hairs upon it with a little saliva and applied it to one of the cracks of the door. Then approaching the window, near which Thaïs stood peaceful and contented, he fell on his knees, praised God three times, and cried:

"How amiable is she who walks in the paths of life! How lovely are her feet and resplendent her face!"

He rose, lowered his hood over his eyes, and slowly departed.

Albina called one of the virgins.

"Daughter," said she, "take Thaïs all she needs: bread, water, and a three-holed flute."

III

THE EUPHORBIUM

THE EUPHORBIUM

PAPHNUTIUS was on his way back to the holy desert. He had embarked at Athribis, upon the boat which ascended the Nile to carry provisions to the monastery of the Abbot Serapion. When he disembarked, his disciples advanced to meet him with great demonstrations of joy. Some raised their hands to heaven, others, prostrate upon the earth, kissed the priest's sandals. For they already knew what he had accomplished in Alexandria. In the same way the monks usually received secretly and rapidly news concerning the safety or glory of the Church. News spread through the desert with the rapidity of a simoom.

While Paphnutius plowed through the sand, his disciples followed him, praising God. Flavian, who was the eldest of the brethren, was suddenly seized with pious delirium and began to sing an inspired canticle.

When they reached the threshold of their master's hut, they all knelt and said:

"Will our father bless us and give us each a measure of oil to feast at his return?"

Paul the Simple alone remained standing and asked: "Who is this man?" not recognizing Paphnutius. But no one noticed him, for he was known to be without intelligence, though full of piety.

The priest of Antinoë alone in his hut thought: "I have at last regained the asylum of my rest and felicity. I have returned to the citadel of my content. Whence comes it that this dear roof of reeds does not receive me as a friend, and that the walls do not say: 'Welcome!' Nothing, since my departure, has changed in this my chosen dwelling. Here is my table and bed. Here is the mummy's head which so often inspired me with salutary thoughts, and there is the book in which I have often sought the images of God. Yet I can find nothing of what I left. Things appear despoiled of their customary grace, and I seem to see them to-day for the first time. When I look at this table and couch, which I years ago made with my own hands, this black and withered head, these rolls of papyrus covered with the words of God, I seem to see the relics of a dead man. After knowing them so well, I no longer recognize them. Alas, since nothing around me is really changed, it is I who am no longer what I was. I am another. The dead man was myself. What has he become, O God? What has he carried away? What has he left me? And who am I?"

He was particularly uneasy at finding that his hut was small, when, considering it with the eyes of faith, it should have seemed immense, since the infinite of God commenced there.

When he began to pray with his forehead upon the earth, he partly recovered his joyfulness. Hardly an hour passed in prayer before the image of Thaïs stood before his eyes. He returned thanks to God:

"Jesus, it is thou who sendeth her to me. I recognize thy immense goodness: thou wishest me to be pleased, assured, and calmed by the sight of her whom I have given thee. Thou presentest before mine eyes her harmless smile, her innocent grace, her beauty from which I have plucked the sting. To flatter me, Lord, thou showest her to me, such as I have adorned and purified in thy intent, as one friend recalls with a smile to another the agreeable present he has received. For this reason I see this woman with pleasure, sure that her vision comes from thee. Thou desirest not to forget I have given her thee, Jesus. Keep her, since she pleases thee, and do not let her charms shine for others as for thee."

During the whole night he could not sleep, and saw Thaïs more distinctly than he had seen her in the Nymphs' grotto. He bore witness to himself, saying:

"What I did, I did for the glory of God."

But, to his great surprise, he had no peace in his heart. He sighed:

"Why art thou sad, O my soul, and why art thou disquieted within me?"

His soul remained uneasy. He was thirty days in the state of sadness, which to the hermit presages horrible trials. The image of Thaïs did not leave him night or day. He did not drive it away, because he still thought it came from God and was the image of a saint. But one morning she visited him in a dream, with her hair crowned with violets, and was so redoubtable in her sweetness, that he cried out with fright and awoke covered with cold sweat. While his eyes were still blinking with sleep, he felt a warm damp breath upon his face: a little jackal, with its two paws placed upon the head of the bed, blew its stinking breath at him and laughed from the bottom of its throat.

Paphnutius was greatly astonished at this, and felt as if a tower was sinking beneath his feet. In fact he fell from the summit of his lost confidence. For some time he was incapable of thought; then, recovering his senses, his meditations only served to increase his uneasiness.

"There are two explanations," he said to himself. "One is that this vision, like the preceding ones, comes from God; it was good, and my natural perversity has spoiled it, as wine turns sour in a dirty glass. I have, by my unworthiness, changed edification into scandal, and the devil's jackal has at once obtained a great advantage. The other is, that this vision did not come from God, but from the devil, and was evil. In this case, I doubt whether the preceding ones had, as I believed them to have, a celestial origin. I am, in that case, incapable of that kind of discernment necessary to an ascetic. In both cases, God shows his estrangement from me, and I feel its effect, without being able to explain the cause."

He reasoned in this way, and prayed in anguish:

"O just God, for what trials dost thou reserve thy servant, if the apparitions of thy saints are a danger to them? Make me to know, by an intelligible sign, what comes from thee, and what from the other."

As God, whose designs are impenetrable, did not judge it necessary to enlighten his servant, Paphnutius, plunged into doubt, resolved to think no more of Thaïs. But his resolution was barren. The absent one was upon him. She looked at him while he was reading, meditating, praying, or in contemplation. Her ideal approach was preceded by a slight noise, like the rustling of a woman's robe, and these visions had an exactitude not presented by realities, which are themselves moving and confused, while phantoms proceeding from solitude bear their most marked characteristics, and present an all powerful fixity. She came to him in various shapes; sometimes pensive, her forehead crowned with her last perishable crown, clad, as at the banquet of Alexandria, in a mauve-colored robe, embroidered with silver flowers; sometimes voluptuous, in a cloud of airy gauze, and bathed in the warm shadows of the Nymphs' grotto; sometimes pious and radiant in the sackcloth of celestial joy; sometimes tragic, her eyes swimming with the horror of death, and showing her naked breast, covered with the blood of her broken heart. The most disturbing part of these visions to him was the return of crowns, tunics, and veils, which he had burned with his own hands; it became evident to him that these things had an indestructible soul, and he cried:

"Here are the countless souls of the sins of Thaïs come to me!"

When he turned his head he felt Thaïs behind him, and was still more uneasy. His misery was cruel. But as his soul and body remained pure in the midst of temptation, he hoped in God and reproached him tenderly.

"My God, if I went so far to seek her among the Gentiles, it was for thee, not for myself. It would not be right for me to suffer for what I did in thy interest. Protect me, gentle Jesus! My Saviour, rescue me! Do not permit the phantom to accomplish that which the body has failed to do. Having triumphed over the flesh, do not allow the shadow to confound me. I know that I am now exposed to greater dangers than ever before. I know by experience that the dream has more power than the reality. How could it be otherwise, since it is itself a superior reality? It is the soul. Plato himself, though he was but an idolater, recognized the real existence of ideas. At that banquet of demons, to which thou accompanied me, Lord, I heard men, it is true, soiled with crime, but certainly not void of intelligence, agree in recognizing that the things we perceive in solitude, meditation, and ecstasy are real, and thy Scriptures, O God, bear witness many times to the virtue of dreams, and the power of visions formed either by thyself, thou splendid God, or by thine adversary."

A new man was in him now he reasoned with God, and God did not hasten to enlighten him. His nights were one long dream, and his days were not distinguishable from his nights. One morning he awoke uttering sighs like those which, in the light of the moon, issue from the tombs of the victims of crime. Thaïs had come displaying her bleeding feet, and while he wept she had glided into his bed. He remained no longer in doubt; the image of Thaïs was an impure one.

His heart revolting with disgust, he rose from his soiled couch, and hid his face in his hands to shade it from the light of day. The hours passed without removing his shame. In his hut all was silent. For the first time for many days Paphnutius was alone. The phantom had at last left him; but its absence even was fearful to him. There was nothing

to distract his attention from the recollection of the dream.
He thought in horror:

"Why did I not repulse it? Why did I not tear myself
from its cold arms and burning knees?"

He dared not pronounce God's name near that abominable
couch, and he feared that, as his hut was so profane, the
demons would enter it at all hours. His fears were not without foundation. Seven little jackals, hardly stopping at the
door, entered in single file, and squatted beneath his bed. At
the hour of vespers an eighth came, whose smell was infec-
tious. The next day a ninth joined the others, and soon there
were thirty, then sixty, then eighty. They became smaller as
they multiplied, and though they were only the size of rats
they covered the floor, the bed, and the stool. One of them
leaped upon the wooden shelf at the head of the bed, and,
putting its forepaws upon the mummy's head, looked at the
monk with eyes of fire. Each day fresh jackals appeared.

To expiate the abomination of his dreams, and rid himself
of impure thoughts, Paphnutius resolved to leave his hut,
which was now unclean, and go into the heart of the desert,
and there give himself up to wonderful austerities, singular
labors, and new penance. But before doing so he visited the
old man Palemon to ask his advice.

He found him in his garden watering his lettuce. It was
sunset. The blue Nile flowed at the foot of the violet hills.
The good man was walking gently, so as not to disturb a dove
which had settled upon his shoulders.

"The Lord be with you," said he, "brother Paphnutius.
Admire his goodness. He sends me beasts he has created, so
that I may talk to them of his works, and so that I may
glorify him in the birds of the air. Look at this dove, notice
the changing clouds of its neck, and tell me if it is not a beautiful work of God. But have you not, brother, to talk to
me upon some holy subject? If so, I will put down my watering pot and listen."

Paphnutius told the old man of his journey, his return, his visions in the day, and his dreams at night, without omitting the criminal dream and the host of jackals.

"Do you not think, father," added he, "that I must hide in the desert, so as to accomplish extraordinary labors and astonish the devil by my austerity?"

"I am only a poor sinner," Palemon replied, "and I know men ill, having passed all my life in this garden with gazelles, hares, and pigeons. But it seems to me, brother, that your malady arises from passing without caution from the agitation of the world to the calm of the desert. These quick changes cannot but impair the health of your soul. You are, brother, like a man who exposes himself in a short time to great heat and cold. A cough is wracking you and fever is tormenting you. In your place, brother Paphnutius, far from immediately withdrawing to some frightful desert, I would have the distractions suitable for a monk and holy priest. I would visit the monasteries in the neighborhood. Some of them are admirable, according to report. That of Serapion contains, I have been told, one thousand four hundred and thirty-two cells. Monks are there divided into as many legions as there are letters in the Greek alphabet. I am assured, too, that certain resemblances between the characters of the monks and the figures of the letters which designate them, are observed, and that, as an example, those who are placed under the letter 'z' have uncertain characters, while those ranged under the letter 'i' have a perfectly upright mind. If I were in your place, brother, I should go and assure myself of this with my own eyes, and I should have no rest till I had contemplated such a wonderful sight. I should not fail to study the constitutions of the different communities scattered on the banks of the Nile, so as to be able to compare them. Those are duties fit for a priest such as you. You have heard that Ephrem the abbot has drawn up spiritual rules of great beauty. With his permission, you, who are a skillful scribe, could copy them. I could not; for my hands, used to the spade, would not have the suppleness necessary to direct the writer's fine reed over the papyrus. But, brother, you possess a knowledge of letters, and you must thank God for it, for good writing cannot be too much admired. The work of copyist and reader is the greatest safeguard against evil thoughts. Brother Paphnutius, why not write down the words of our fathers Paul and Anthony? Little by little in these pious labors you will recover your peace of soul and mind; solitude will become beautiful to you once more, and you will soon be in a fit state of mind to resume the ascetic labors you performed before your voyage interrupted them. In the days when our father Anthony was among us he used to say: 'Excess of fasting produces weakness, and weakness engenders inertia. Some monks ruin their bodies by indiscreetly prolonged fasting. Of them it might be said, "They plunge a dagger into their breast and hand themselves over to the demon's power." ' Thus spake the holy man Anthony; I am but an ignorant man, but by God's grace I have retained our father's word."

Paphnutius thanked Palemon, and promised to meditate upon his advice. After crossing the reed fence which surrounded the little garden, he turned back and saw the gardener watering his lettuce with the dove upon his bent back. At this sight he felt a desire to weep.

Returning to his hut, he found a strange swarm there. It seemed like grains of sand driven by a furious wind, but he recognized it to be myriads of little jackals. This night he saw in a dream a lofty stone column, surmounted by a human figure, and he heard a voice say:

"Mount this column!"

On awakening, persuaded that the dream came to him from heaven, he assembled his disciples and spoke to them thus:

"Well-beloved sons, I leave you to go whither God sends

me. In my absence obey Flavian as if he were myself, and
take care of our brother Paul. My blessing be upon you all.
Adieu."

While he walked away, they remained prostrate, and when
they rose they could see his great black form on the horizon
of sand.

He walked day and night, till he reached the ruins of that
temple built by idolaters, in which he had slept, amid scorpions and sirens, when on his wonderful voyage. The walls
covered with magic symbols were still standing. Thirty gi-
gantic shafts, terminating in human heads or lotus flowers,
still supported enormous stones. Standing alone at the end
of the temple, one of these columns had shaken itself free
from its former burden. It had as a capital a woman's smiling
head, with long eyes, round cheeks, and on the forehead the
horns of a cow.

When Paphnutius saw it, he recognized it as the column
which had been shown him in his dream, and guessed its
height to be thirty-two cubits. Entering the nearest village,
he had a ladder made of that height, and when it was placed
against the column he mounted, knelt upon the capital,
and said to the Lord:

"Here then, O Lord, is the dwelling thou hast chosen me.
Can I remain here in thy grace till the hour of my death?"

He had taken no provisions, committing himself to divine
Providence, and counting upon receiving from the charitable
peasants sufficient for life. On the morrow, towards the hour
of prayer, women and children came, bringing dates and fresh
water, which the little boys took up to the top of the
column.

The capital was not large enough for the monk to extend
his limbs, so he slept with his legs crossed and his head upon
his breast, such sleep being more cruel fatigue to him than
watching. At dawn the hawks flapped him with their wings,
and he awoke full of anguish and fear.

It happened that the carpenter who had made the ladder, feared God. Moved at the thought that the holy man was exposed to sun and rain, and fearing that he would fall from the column in his sleep, the pious man built a roof and railing to it.

The fame, however, of such a marvelous existence spread from village to village, and the laborers of the valley came on the Sabbath, with their wives and children, to contemplate the Stylite.

The disciples of Paphnutius, learning the situation of his sublime retreat, assembled near him, and obtained permission from him to build huts at the foot of the column. Each morning they came and stood in a circle around their master, and listened to his words of wisdom.

"My sons," he said to them, "remain like the little children Jesus loved. In that is salvation. The sin of the flesh is the source and beginning of all sins; they spring from it as from a father. Pride, avarice, idleness, anger, and envy are its beloved children. I will tell you what I saw at Alexandria; I saw the rich carried away by the vice of luxury, which, like a muddy river, washed them into the salt sea."

The abbots Ephrem and Serapion, when informed of this new penance, wished to see it with their own eyes. Sighting in the distance the sail which was bringing them towards him, Paphnutius could not help thinking that God had placed him there as an example to the hermits. At sight of him the two holy abbots did not dissimulate their surprise; after consulting together they, with one accord, began to blame so extraordinary a penance, and exhorted Paphnutius to descend.

"Such a life," said they, "is contrary to all custom; it is singular, and beyond all rules."

Paphnutius replied to them:

"What is monachal life but a life of wonders? Must not a monk's works be as singular as himself? A sign from God has caused me to ascend here; a sign from God will make me descend."

Every day monks came in troops to join the disciples of Paphnutius, and built themselves shelters around the aërial hermitage. Some of them, in imitation of the holy man, ascended other parts of the ruins; but when chided by their brethren, and worn out with fatigue, they soon descended.

Pilgrims flocked from all parts. Some came from afar, and were hungry and thirsty. A poor widow conceived the idea of selling fresh water and melons to them. Leaning upon the column with her red earthen jars, her cups and fruit beneath a blue and white striped awning behind her, she shouted: "Who desires to drink?" Following her example, a baker brought bricks and built an oven, hoping to sell bread and cakes to the strangers. As the crowd of visitors increased without ceasing, and the inhabitants of the great cities of Egypt began to arrive, a man desiring to make money, built a caravansary to lodge masters and their servants, camels and mules. Soon a market sprung up before the column, to which the fishermen of the Nile brought their fish, and the gardeners their vegetables. A barber, who shaved in the open air, enlivened the crowd by his cheery conversation. The old temple, so long enveloped in silence and peace, was full of motion and the countless rumors of life. Innkeepers transformed caves into subterranean halls, and nailed to their ancient pillars notices surmounted by the image of the holy man Paphnutius, and bearing the inscription in Greek and Egyptian: "Pomegranate wine, fig wine, and the real Cilician beer, sold here." Upon the walls sculptured with pure and slender profiles, merchants hung ropes of onions, smoked fish, dead hares, and skinned sheep. In the evening the rats, ancient guests of the ruins, fled in a long file towards the river, while the uneasy ibis stretched their necks as they placed uncertain feet upon the lofty cornices, towards which rose the smoke of kitchens, the shouts of the drinkers, and the cries of the servants.

All around surveyors traced out streets, and masons built convents, chapels, and churches. At the end of six months a town had risen, having a bodyguard, tribunal, prison, and school kept by an old blind scribe.

The pilgrims were without number. Bishops and church dignitaries hastened there full of admiration. The Patriarch of Antioch, who was then in Egypt, came with all his clergy. He highly approved of the extraordinary conduct of the Stylite, and the heads of the churches of Lybia, in the absence of Athanasius, agreed with the Patriarch. Learning this, the abbots Ephrem and Serapion came to excuse themselves for their former condemnation. Paphnutius replied to them:

"Brethren, understand that the penance I endure is hardly equal to the temptations which are sent me, the number and strength of which astound me. A man viewed from the outside is small, and from the top of the socle, whither God has borne me, I see human beings moving like mice. But, considered internally, man is immense; he is as great as the world, for he contains it. All that extends before me, these monasteries, hostelries, barques upon the river, and villages, and the fields, canals, sand, and mountains, which I see in the distance, are as nothing compared with what is in me. I bear in my heart innumerable cities and illimitable deserts. Evil and death stretch over this immensity, cover it as the night covers the earth. I am in myself alone a universe of evil thoughts."

He spoke thus because the desire of women was in him.

In the seventh month, there came from Alexandria, Bubastis, and Sais, women who, though long barren, hoped to obtain children through the holy man's intercession, and the virtue of the column. They rubbed their barren flanks against the stone. Then, as far as the eye could reach, came chariots and litters, which stopped and crowded beneath the man of God. Out of them came sick people frightful to look upon. Mothers presented to Paphnutius their young children, whose limbs were curved, eyes blind, mouths foaming, and voices harsh. He placed his hands upon them. The blind approached him with waving arms, and raised at hazard towards him their faces pierced with two bleeding holes. Paralytics showed him the perfect immobility, the mortal withering, and the hideous contraction of their members; the halt presented to his view their clubfeet; women with cancers uncovered before him breasts which were being devoured by the invisible vulture. Dropsical women were placed upon the earth at his feet. He blessed them all. Nubians, attacked by elephantine leprosy, advanced with heavy tread, and peered at him with weeping eyes from an inanimate face. He made the sign of the Cross upon them. They brought him upon a litter a young girl from Aphroditopolis, who, after vomiting blood, slept for three days. She seemed like a waxen image, and her parents, who believed her to be dead, had placed a palm upon her breast. Paphnutius prayed to God, and the young girl raised her head, and opened her eyes.

As the miracles worked by the holy man were published abroad, the unfortunate people, attacked by the disease which the Greeks call the divine malady, hastened to him from all parts of Egypt in countless legions. As soon as they perceived the column they were seized with convulsions, rolled upon the earth, went into a frenzy; curled themselves into a ball. His disciples, and this is almost incredible, agitated by violent delirium, imitated the contortions of epileptics. Monks and pilgrims, men and women, wallowed and writhed pell-mell, with twisted limbs and foaming mouths, swallowing handfuls of earth and prophesying. Paphnutius from the top of his column felt a tremor run through his limbs, and cried to God:

"I am the scapegoat, and I take upon me all the impurities of this people, and for that reason, Lord, is my body filled with evil spirits."

Each time a sick person went away cured, the disciples shouted, without ceasing, as they bore him in triumph:

"We have just seen another fountain of Siloe!"

Already hundreds of crutches hung from the miraculous column; thankful women, too, hung crowns and votive images upon it. Greeks traced upon it ingenious distiches, and, as each pilgrim engraved his name upon the stone, it was soon covered to a man's height with an infinity of Latin, Greek, Coptic, Punic, Hebrew, Syriac and magic characters.

When the feast of Easter came, there was in the city of miracles such a crowd of people that the elderly believed themselves taken back to the days of the ancient mysteries. Upon a vast plain the speckled robes of the Egyptians mingled with the burnus of the Arabs, the white cotton of the Nubians, the short cloak of the Greeks, the toga with long folds of the Romans, and the scarlet robes of the barbarians. Veiled women passed by on their donkeys, preceded by black eunuchs, who cleared a way for them with blows of their staves. Acrobats, stretching a carpet upon the ground, did feats of skill, and wriggled elegantly before a circle of silent spectators. Snake charmers unrolled living girdles from their outstretched arms. This mighty crowd shone, glittered, made a dust, jingled, shouted, and grumbled. The imprecations of camel drivers, as they struck their beasts, the cries of merchants, who sold charms against leprosy and evil eye, the chanting of verses from the Scriptures by monks, the moaning of women in the prophetic crises, the yelping of mendicants as they repeated ancient harem songs, the bleating of sheep, and braying of donkeys, the shouts of sailors to tardy passengers, all mingled made an immense hubbub, and this dominated even the strident voices of little naked negroes who were running here and there offering fresh dates for sale.

All these diverse beings were stifling under the white sky, in a thick atmosphere loaded with the perfume of women, the odor of negroes, the smoke of cooking, the vapors of the gums, which the pious bought of shepherds to burn before the holy man.

At night fires, torches, and lanterns were lit on all sides, and everything was red shadow and black form. Upright, in the midst of a circle of crouching listeners, an old man, his face lit up by a smoky lamp, told how once Bitiou enchanted his heart, snatched it from his breast, put it in an acacia, and then changed himself into a tree. He made gestures, which his shadow repeated with laughable deformations, and the wonder-stricken audience uttered cries of admiration. In the inns, the drinkers, reclining upon divans, called for beer or wine. Dancers, with painted eyes and naked breasts, performed before them religious and lascivious scenes. Young men played dice apart, and old men pursued courtesans. Above these moving forms the motionless column stood alone; the horned head looked into the shadow, and above it Paphnutius watched between heaven and earth. Suddenly the moon arose above the Nile, like the naked shoulder of a goddess. The hills streamed with light and azure, and Paphnutius thought he saw the flesh of Thaïs sparkling in the light of the waters among the sapphires of the night.

The days passed, but the holy man remained upon the column. When the rainy season came the water from heaven, passing through the cracks of the roof, inundated his body; his benumbed limbs became still more incapable of motion. Burned by the sun and colored by the dew, his skin began to crack; large ulcers ate up his arms and legs. But the desire of Thaïs consumed him within, and he cried:

"Is it not enough, O God of Power! More temptations! More unclean thoughts! More monstrous desires! Lord, pass into me the whole luxury of men, so that I may expiate it all! If it is false that the bitch of Argos has taken upon herself the sins of the world, as I heard certain forgers of impostures say, still this fable contains a hidden sense, the exactness of which I recognize to-day. For it is true that the infamies of the people enter into the souls of the saints to be there engulfed as in an abyss. So the souls of the just are soiled with more mire than the souls of sinners ever contain. Therefore I glorify thee, my God, for making me the sink of the universe."

But one day a great rumor spread in the holy city, and even rose to the ears of the ascetic: a great personage, a most illustrious man, the prefect of the fleet of Alexandria, Lucius Aurelius Cotta, was coming, is coming, is approaching!

The news was true. Old Cotta, who was setting out to inspect the canals and the navigation of the Nile, had several times experienced a desire to see the Stylite and the new city, which had received the name of Stylopolis. One morning the Stylopolitans saw the river covered with sails. Cotta approached on board a gilded galley, hung with purple, followed by his flotilla. He landed, and advanced, accompanied by his secretary, who bore his tablets, and Aristeus his doctor, with whom he loved to converse.

A numerous suite followed him, and the bank was bright with arms and military uniforms. He stopped a few paces from the column and began to examine the Stylite, wiping his face with his toga. Of a naturally curious disposition, he had in his long voyages observed much. He loved to recall, and meditated writing, after his Punic history, a book upon the singular things he had seen. He seemed much interested in the sight before him.

"How strange," said he, blowing and sweating. "And a circumstance worthy of note is, that this man has been my guest. Yes, this man came to sup with me a year ago; after that he carried off an actress."

And, turning to his secretary, he said: "Note that, child,

upon my tablets; as well as the column's dimensions, without forgetting the form of the capital."

Then wiping his forehead once more, he said:

"Well-informed persons have told me that since our monk mounted this column a year ago, he has not left it for a moment. Aristeus, is that possible?"

"It is possible to a fool and a sick man," replied Aristeus, "but would be impossible to a man who was healthy in body and mind. Do you not know, Lucius, that sometimes maladies of the soul and body communicate to those who are afflicted by them powers which healthy men do not possess? To tell the truth, neither good nor bad health really exists. There is only different states of the organs. From studying what are called maladies, I have come to consider them as necessary forms of life. I take more pleasure in studying them than in combating them. There are some which cannot be observed without admiration, and which conceal under apparent disorder profound harmonies, and quartan ague is indeed a very beautiful thing! Sometimes certain maladies of the body determine the exaltation of the faculties of the mind. You know Creon. As a child he was stupid, and stuttered. But after hurting his head by falling down a staircase, he became the skillful lawyer whom you know. This monk must be afflicted in some concealed organ. Besides, his kind of existence is not quite as singular as it seems to you, Lucius. Recall the gymnosophists of India, who can remain entirely motionless not only for one year, but for twenty, thirty, and even forty years."

"By Jupiter," replied Cotta, "that is a great aberration! For man is born to act, and inertia is an unpardonable crime, since it is committed to the prejudice of the state. I don't quite know to what belief to attach so fatal a practice. It is likely that certain Asiatic creeds are responsible for it. At the time I was Governor of Syria, I saw the phalli erected in the city of Hera. A man mounted these twice a year, and remained for seven days. The people are convinced that this man obtains the prosperity of Syria by thus conversing with the gods. This custom seemed to me to be void of reason; but I did nothing to injure it. For I think that a functionary ought not to abolish the customs of the people, but, on the contrary, ought to assure their observance. It is not the duty of the government to impose creeds; its duty is to give satisfaction to those which exist, and which, good or bad, have been determined by the spirit of the times, places, and races. If it undertakes to combat them, it shows itself revolutionary in spirit, tyrannical in action, and is rightly detested. Besides, what other way is there to rise above vulgar superstitions than to tolerate and understand them? Aristeus, my advice is to leave the dreamer at peace in the air, exposed only to the attacks of the birds. It is not by doing violence to him that I will take advantage of him, but by rendering account to myself of his thoughts and creed."

He panted, coughed, and placing his hand upon his secretary's shoulder, said:

"Child, note that in certain sects of the Christians it is good to carry off courtesans and to live upon columns. You can add that these customs suppose the cult of lustful deities. But in this particular we must ask the man himself."

Then, raising his head and shading his eyes from the sun with his hand, he shouted:

"Paphnutius! If you remember that you were my guest, answer me. What are you doing there? Why did you ascend, and why do you remain there? Has this column phallic significance in your mind?"

Paphnutius, considering Cotta to be an idolater, did not deign to reply. But Flavian, his disciple, approaching, said:

"Most noble lord, this holy man takes the sins of the world upon him and cures its maladies."

"By Jupiter, do you hear that, Aristeus?" cried Cotta.

"The dreamer practices medicine like you. What do you say of so exalted a brother physician?"

Aristeus shook his head, saying:

"It is possible that he cures better than I do certain maladies, such as epilepsy, commonly called the divine malady, although all maladies are equally divine, for they all come from the gods. But the cause of this disease is partly in the imagination, and you will see, Lucius, that this monk thus perched upon the head of the goddess appeals more forcibly to the imagination of the sick than I know how to do, bent as I am, in my laboratory, over my mortars and phials. There are, Lucius, certain forces infinitely more powerful than reason and science.

"Which?" asked Cotta.

"Ignorance and folly," replied Aristeus.

"I have rarely seen anything more curious than this sight," replied Cotta, "and I hope that some day a clever writer will tell the story of the founding of Stylopolis. But even the rarest sights must not detain a grave and laborious man longer than absolutely necessary. Let us go and inspect the canals. Adieu, Paphnutius! or, rather, *au revoir!* If ever you descend to earth and return to Alexandria, do not fail, I beg you, to come and sup with me."

These words which were heard by the disciples ran from mouth to mouth, and as they were spread abroad by the faithful, added incomparable splendor to the glory of Paphnutius. Pious imaginations adorned and transformed them, and it was said that the holy man had, from the top of the column, converted the prefect of the fleet to the faith of the apostles and fathers of Nicæa. The faithful gave to the last words of Aurelius Cotta a figurative meaning; in their mouths the supper, to which this personage had invited the ascetic, became a holy communion, a spiritual love feast, a celestial banquet. This story became embellished with many marvelous circumstances, which the inventors themselves were the first to believe. They said that at the moment Cotta, after a long argument, confessed the truth, an angel came from heaven to wipe the sweat from his forehead. They added that his secretary and doctor were also converted. When the miracle became notorious, the deacons of the principal churches of Lybia wrote it down as authentic. From that time it may be said, without exaggeration, that the entire world was seized with a desire to visit Paphnutius, and that in the Occident, as well as in the Orient, every Christian turned on him his dazzled eyes. The most illustrious cities in Italy sent ambassadors to him, and the Roman Cæsar, the divine Constans, who upheld Christian orthodoxy, wrote him a letter which his ambassadors presented with great ceremony. Now one night, while the city stretched at his feet slept in the dew, he heard a voice saying:

"Paphnutius, you are famous for your works, and powerful in your words. God has raised you up for his glory. He has chosen you to work miracles, cure the sick, convert Pagans, enlighten the fishermen, confound the Aryans and reestablish the peace of the Church."

Paphnutius replied:

"God's will be done!"

The voice replied:

"Arise, go seek the impious Constantius in his palace, for he, instead of imitating the wisdom of his brother Constans, favors the error of Arius and Marcus. Go! The gates of brass shall open before you, and your sandals shall ring upon the golden pavement of the basilicas, before the throne of the Cæsars, and your terrible voice shall change the heart of the son of Constantine. You shall rule over the pacified and powerful Church. And in the same way that the soul directs the body, the Church shall govern the Empire. You shall be placed over senators, counts, and patricians. You shall make the people's hunger and the audacity of the barbarians cease. Old Cotta, knowing you to be ruler, shall seek the honor of

washing your feet. At your death your robe shall be taken
to the Patriarch of Alexandria, and great Athanasius, grown
gray in his glory, shall kiss it as the relic of a saint. Go!"
Paphnutius replied:
"God's will be done!"
Making an effort to stand upright, he prepared to descend.
But the voice, divining his idea, said to him:
"Do not descend by the ladder. It would be acting as an
ordinary man, and disregarding the gifts which are in you.
Estimate your power better, angelic Paphnutius. A saint as
holy as you should fly through the air. Leap; the angels are
there to sustain you. Leap."
Paphnutius replied:
"May God's will reign on earth as in heaven!"
Balancing his long arms, outstretched like the featherless
wings of a great sick bird, he was about to jump, when sud-
denly a hideous sneering laugh sounded in his ear. In fear
he asked:
"Who is laughing like that?"
"Ah, ah," yelped the voice, "we are not yet at the end of
our friendship; you will some day become more intimately
acquainted with me. Dear friend, it was I who made you
mount here, and I must express my entire satisfaction at the
docility with which you have obeyed my wishes. Paphnutius,
I am satisfied with you."
Paphnutius murmured, with a voice choking with fear:
"Get thee behind me! I recognize you: you are he who
bore Jesus to the pinnacle of the Temple, and showed him
all the realms of this world."
He fell back upon the stone in despair. "Why did I not
recognize you before?" he thought. "More miserable than
those blind, deaf, and paralytics who hope in me, I have lost
the sense of the supernatural things, and, more depraved than
the maniacs, who eat the earth, and approach corpses, I can
no longer distinguish the clamors of hell from the voices of

heaven. I have lost even the discernment of the new-born babe, who weeps when taken from his nurse's breast, of the dog which tracks its master by its scent, and of the plant which turns towards the sun. I am the plaything of the devils. So it was Satan who brought me here. When he placed me upon this pinnacle, luxury and pride mounted by my side. It is not the magnitude of my temptations which dismays me. Anthony upon his mountain endured the like. I desire their swords to pierce my flesh under the angels' gaze. I have even succeeded in cherishing my tortures. But God is silent, and his silence astounds me. He leaves me, who have only him; he leaves me alone in the horror of his absence. He flies from me. I desire to run after him. This stone burns my feet. Quick, let me depart, let me overtake God."

Immediately he seized the ladder which remained leaning against the side of the column, placed his foot upon it, and descending a step, found himself face to face with the beast's head: it smiled strangely. He was certain that the place he had taken for the seat of his repose and glory was only the diabolical instrument of his trouble and damnation. He hastily descended to the ground. His feet had forgotten the earth; his legs trembled. But feeling the shadow of the cursed column upon him he forced himself to run. Everyone slept. He traversed, without being seen, the great square surrounded by inns, hostelries, and caravansaries, and rushed down a lane leading towards the Lybian hills. A dog, which pursued him, barking, only stopped at the edge of the sand. Paphnutius fled through a country whose only roads are the tracks of wild beasts. Leaving behind him huts abandoned by coiners of bad money, he continued his desolate flight all through the next and the next day.

At last, almost dying of hunger, thirst, and fatigue, and not yet knowing whether God was afar, he discovered a mute city, which stretched right and left, and was lost in the

purple of the horizon. The dwelling places far apart, and all
alike, resembled pyramids cut down to half their height.
They were tombs. The gates were broken down, and out of
the shadow of the halls shone the eyes of hyenas and wolves
which were feeding their cubs, while upon the threshold lay
the bodies of the dead, despoiled by brigands and gnawed
by beasts. Crossing this city of the dead, Paphnutius fell ex-
hausted before a tomb standing apart near a spring crowned
with palm trees. This tomb was very ornate, and, as there
was no gate, from without a chamber could be seen full of
coiled serpents.

"There is," he sighed, "my chosen dwelling, the tabernacle
of my repentance and penitence."

He crawled inside, drove away the reptiles with his foot,
and remained prostrate upon the stones for eighteen hours, at
the end of which he went to the fountain and drank from
the palm of his hand. Then he gathered dates and a few
twigs of lotus, the seeds of which he ate. Thinking that this
kind of life was good, he made it the rule of his existence.
From morning till evening he did not raise his forehead from
the stones.

One day, while he was thus prostrate, he heard a voice
saying:

"Gaze at those images and learn."

Then, raising his head, he saw upon the walls of the chamber paintings representing laughable and familiar scenes. It
was a very ancient work of marvelous exactitude. There were
cooks blowing the fire with inflated cheeks; others were
plucking geese, or cooking joints of mutton in pots. Further
on, a huntsman was carrying on his shoulders a gazelle,
pierced with arrows. Then there were peasants engaged in
sowing and harvesting. Elsewhere were women dancing to
the music of violins, flutes, and harps. A young girl was playing the theorbo. A lotus flower shone in her black and finely
plaited hair. Her transparent robe showed the pure outline

of her body. Her breasts and mouth were like flowers. Her beautiful eyes looked out from an exquisitely turned profile. Her figure was exquisite. Paphnutius looked at her, lowered his eyes, and replied to the voice:

"Why do you order me to look at those images? Without a doubt, they represent the terrestrial days of the idolater whose body reposes under my feet at the bottom of a shaft in a grave of black basalt. They recall the life of a dead man, and are, in spite of their brilliant colors, the shades of a shade. The life of a dead man! O vanity!"

"He is dead, but he has lived," replied the voice, "and you will die, and you will not have lived."

From that day Paphnutius had not a moment's rest. The voice spoke to him without ceasing. The theorbo player looked at him fixedly from beneath her long lashes. In her turn she spoke:

"See, I am mysterious and beautiful. Love me; exhaust in my arms the love which torments you. Of what use will be your fear? You cannot escape me; I am the beauty of woman. Whither do you think of fleeing, madman? You will find my image in the beauty of flowers, in the grace of palms, in the flight of doves, in the bounds of gazelles, in the undulating course of streams, in the soft light of the moon, and, if you close your eyes, you will find it in yourself. A thousand years ago the man who sleeps here encircled with bandages upon a bed of black stone pressed me to his breast. A thousand years ago he received his last kiss from my mouth, and his sleep is still perfumed by it. You know me well, Paphnutius. Why did you not recognize me? I am one of the countless incarnations of Thaïs. You are a learned monk, and well advanced in knowledge. You have traveled, and travel teaches most. Often a day passed abroad brings more novelties than ten years spent at home. Now you must have heard that Thaïs lived formerly in Argos, under the name of Helen. She had another existence in Thebes Hecatompylos.

Thaïs of Thebes was myself. Why did you not divine that? I have in my lifetime taken part in most of the sins of the world, and now, though but a shade, I am still capable of being a partner in your sins, beloved monk. Why were you surprised? Everywhere you go, you will be certain to find Thaïs."

He struck his forehead upon the stones and cried out in fright. Each night the theorbo player quitted the wall, approached, and spoke in a clear voice, which mingled with her cool breath. As the holy man resisted the temptations which she put before him, she said to him:

"Love me; yield, friend. As long as you resist me I will torment you. You do not know a dead woman's patience. I will wait, if it is necessary, till you are dead. Being a sorceress, I can put into your lifeless body a spirit which will reanimate it and which will not refuse me what I have asked of you in vain. Think, Paphnutius, of the strangeness of your situation, when your happy soul shall see from heaven its own body give itself up to sin. Even God, who has promised to return you the body after the last judgment and the consummation of the centuries, will be very much embarrassed! How will he be able to install in celestial glory a human form inhabited by a devil and in the power of a sorceress? You have not thought of this difficulty. Nor, perhaps, has God. Between ourselves, he is not very subtle. The most simple sorceress easily deceives him, and if he had not his thunder and the cataracts of heaven—the brats of the village would pull his beard. He certainly is not so cunning as the old serpent his adversary. The latter is a marvelous artist. My beauty is due to his work upon my attire. It was he who taught me to plait my hair, and make myself rose and agate nails. You have too long disregarded him. When you came to live in this tomb, you drove away the serpents which dwelt here with your foot, without troubling yourself to find out if they were of his family, and you crushed their eggs.

I am afraid, my poor friend, that you are in great danger.
You had, however, been warned that he was a musician and
lover. What did you do? You have fallen out with science
and beauty. You are quite miserable, and Jehovah is not coming to your assistance. It is not likely he will come. Being as
large as all things, he cannot move without space, and if,
impossible though it be, he made the least movement all
creation would be overthrown. Beautiful hermit, he will give
me a kiss."

Paphnutius was not ignorant of the wonders worked by
the magic arts. He thought in his dire distress:

"Perhaps the dead man buried at my feet knows the words
written in that mysterious book which remains concealed not
far from here at the bottom of a royal tomb. By virtue
of those words the dead, resuming the form which they had
when on earth, see the light of the sun and the smile of
women."

His fear was that the theorbo player and the dead man
would embrace, as in life, and that he would see them. Sometimes he thought he heard the light breath of kisses.

Trouble was all round him, and now, in God's absence, he
feared to think, as well as to look.

One evening, when he was prostrate, as his custom was,
an unknown voice said to him:

"Paphnutius, there are more people on earth than you
think, and if I showed you what I have seen, you would die
of fright. There are men with only one eye, that being in
the middle of their forehead. There are men with only one
leg, who hop instead of walking. There are men who change
their sex, and there are women who become men. There are
tree-men, whose roots grow into the earth. There are headless
men, too, who have two eyes, a nose, and mouth in their
chests. Do you, in good faith, believe that Jesus Christ died
for the salvation of these men?"

On another occasion he had a vision. He saw in a bright

light a large causeway, streams, and gardens. Along the causeway Aristobulus and Chereas galloped their Syrian horses, with the love of the chase burning on their cheeks. Under a portico Callicrates declaimed verses; satisfied pride trembled in his voice, and shone from his eyes. In a garden Zenothemis gathered golden apples and caressed an azure-winged serpent. Clad in white, and wearing a sparkling miter, Hermodorus meditated beneath a sacred persea, which bore, instead of flowers, little heads with pure profiles, coifed like Egyptian goddesses, vultures, hawks, or the moon's shining disc, while apart on the edge of a fountain Nicias studied upon a miliary sphere the harmonious movement of the stars.

Then a veiled woman approached the monk, holding in her hand a twig of myrtle. She said to him:

"Look! some seek eternal beauty, and put the infinite into their ephemeral lives. Others live without much care; but by simply yielding to their good nature they are happy and beautiful, and in allowing themselves to live they render glory to the sovereign artist of all, for man is a beautiful hymn of God. They all consider happiness innocent, and joy permissible. Paphnutius, if they were to be right, what a dupe you would be!"

The vision faded.

Thus Paphnutius was tempted without ceasing in body and mind. Satan did not give him a moment's rest. The solitude of this tomb was more thickly peopled than the crossroads of a large city. The demons uttered loud bursts of laughter, and millions of larvæ and lemures performed there the image of the works of life. In the evening when he went to the fountain, satyrs, mingled with fauns, danced around him, and dragged him into their lewd steps. The demons feared him no more. They overwhelmed him with jests, obscene taunts, and blows. One day a devil, not taller than his arm, stole the cord which he used as a girdle.

He murmured:

"Thought, where hast thou led me?"

He resolved to work with his hands, so as to procure for his mind the rest it needed. Near the fountain large-leaved bananas grew in the shade of the palms. He cut off their stalks and carried them into the tomb. There he ground the stalks with a stone, and reduced them to fine filaments, as he had seen the rope makers do; for he proposed to make a cord in place of the one the devil had stolen from him. The demons felt some annoyance; they ceased their noise, and the theorbo player herself, renouncing magic, remained quiet upon the painted wall. Paphnutius, while crushing the banana stalks, confirmed his courage and faith.

"With the assistance of heaven," he said to himself, "I will subdue the flesh. As for the soul, it has retained hope. In vain would the devils and this woman like to inspire me with doubts as to God's nature. I will answer them from the mouth of the apostle John: 'In the beginning was the word, and the word was God.' I firmly believe that, and if it is absurd I then believe it more firmly still. To go further, it must be absurd; if it were not I should not believe it, I should know it. Now, knowledge does not give life; it is faith alone that saves."

He exposed the detached fibers to the sun and dew, but each morning took care to bring them into the tomb to prevent them from rotting, and he rejoiced to feel in himself the rebirth of infant simplicity. When he had woven his cord, he cut the rushes to make mats and baskets. The sepulchral chamber resembled the workshop of a basket maker, and Paphnutius passed easily from work to prayer. God, however, was not favorable to him, for one night he was awakened by a voice which froze him with horror; he divined that it was the voice of the dead man.

The voice uttered a rapid call, a light whisper:

"Helen, Helen, come and bathe with me. Come quickly!"

A woman, whose mouth grazed the monk's ear, replied:

"Friend, I cannot rise; a man is upon me."

Suddenly Paphnutius perceived that his cheek was resting upon a woman's breast. He recognized the theorbo player, who, half freeing herself, raised her breast. Then he embraced desperately this wanton and perfumed flower of the flesh, and consumed with the desire of damnation, he cried:

"Remain, remain, my heaven!"

But she was already standing at the door. She laughed, and the rays of the moon silvered her smile.

"What good shall I do by remaining?" she said. "The shadow of a shadow suffices a lover endowed with an imagination as vivid as yours. Besides, you have sinned. What more do you need?"

Paphnutius wept throughout the night, and when the dawn came he breathed a prayer sweeter than a plaint:

"Jesus, my Jesus, why dost thou leave me? Thou seest the danger which threatens me. Come to my aid, gentle Saviour. Since thy father loves me no longer, since he hears me not, consider that I have only thee. From him to me nothing is possible. I cannot understand him, and he cannot pity me. But thou art born of a woman, that is why I hope in thee. Remember thou art a man. I implore thee, not because thou art God of God, light of light, very God of very God, but because thou hast lived poor and feeble upon this earth where I suffer, because Satan wished to tempt thy flesh, because the sweat of thy agony froze upon thy brow. It is thy humanity I beseech, my Jesus, my brother Jesus!"

After praying thus, and wringing his hands, a formidable burst of laughter shook the walls of the tomb, and the voice which had sounded on the summit of the column said, with a sneer:

"That is a prayer worthy of the breviary of Marcus the heretic. Paphnutius is an Aryan. Paphnutius is an Aryan!"

The priest fell lifeless, as if struck by lightning.

.   .   .   .

When he opened his eyes, he saw around him monks in black robes, pouring water on his temples, and reciting exorcisms. Several stood upright, holding palms.

"As we crossed the desert," one of them said, "we heard cries in this tomb, and entering, found you lying inert upon the stones. Without doubt, the demons had knocked you down and fled at our approach."

Paphnutius, raising his head, asked in a weak voice:

"Brethren, who are you? Why are you holding palms in your hands? Is not this in view of my burial?"

They answered him:

"Brother, do you not know that our father Anthony, at the age of one hundred and five years, warned of his approaching end, has descended from Mount Colzin, whither he had retired, and has come to bless the countless children of his soul. We are going with palms to meet our spiritual father. But, brother, how is it that you are ignorant of so great an event? Is it possible that no angel has come to warn you in this tomb?"

"Alas," replied Paphnutius, "I do not deserve such goodness, and the sole guests of this dwelling are demons and vampires. Pray for me! I am Paphnutius, priest of Antinöe, the most miserable of God's servants."

At the name of Paphnutius all, waving their palms, murmured praises. He who had already spoken, cried with admiration:

"Is it possible that you are that holy man Paphnutius, so celebrated in his works, that people think he will some day equal the great Anthony himself? O most venerable, you are the man who converted the courtesan Thaïs, and who, standing upon a lofty column, was carried off by the seraphim. Those who watched during the night at the foot of the column saw your happy assumption. Angels' wings surrounded you in a white cloud, and your extended right hand blessed the dwellings of men. On the morrow, when the people could no longer see you, a long groan rose towards the uncrowned column. But Flavian, your disciple, published abroad the miracle, and assumed the government of the monks in your place. One simple man, named Paul, was the only one who wished to contradict this unanimous sentiment. He was sure that he had seen you in a dream carried off by devils; the crowd wished to stone him, and it is a wonder he escaped death. I am Zozimos, abbot of those hermits who are prostrate at your feet. Like them I kneel before you so that you may bless the father with the children. Then, you shall tell us the wonders which God has deigned to accomplish through your agency."

"Far from favoring me as you believe," replied Paphnutius, "the Lord has tried me by frightful temptations. I was not carried off by angels. But a wall of shadow rose before my eyes and walked before me. I lived in a dream. Without God, everything is a dream. When I made the voyage to Alexandria, I heard many speeches in a few hours, and I knew that the army of error was very numerous. It pursued me, and I am surrounded by swords."

Zozimos replied:

"Venerable father, we must consider that saints, and specially hermit saints, undergo terrible temptations. If you were not carried up to heaven in the arms of the seraphim, it is certain that the Lord has granted this grace to your image, since Flavian, monks and people, were witness of your assumption."

Paphnutius resolved to go and receive Anthony's benediction.

"Brother Zozimos," said he, "give me one of those palms, and let us go to meet our father."

"Let us go," replied Zozimos; "military order suits monks who are above all soldiers. You and I, being abbots, will walk in front. The others shall follow us singing psalms."

They began their march, and Paphnutius said:

"God is unity, for he is the truth, which is one. The world

is diverse, because it is error. A person must turn away from all the spectacles of nature, even those most innocent in appearance. Their diversity, which renders them agreeable, is the sign that they are bad. For that reason I cannot see a bunch of papyrus under the sleeping waters, without my soul being veiled in melancholy. Everything which the senses perceive is detestable. The least grain of sand brings a danger. Each thing tempts us. Woman is simply composed of all the temptations floating in the air, upon the flowering earth, and in the clear waters. Happy is he whose soul is a vast seal! Happy he who knows how to become mute, blind and deaf, and who understands nothing of the world, as to understand God!"

Zozimos, after meditating upon these words, replied as follows:

"Venerable father, it is necessary for me to avow my sins to you, since you have bared your soul to me. So we will confess one another according to apostolic usage. Before becoming a monk, I led an abominable life in the world. At Madaura, a city celebrated for its courtesans, I sought all sorts of love. Each night I supped with young profligates and flute players, and I returned with the one who pleased me most. A saint as yourself would never imagine the fury of my desire. It will suffice for me to say that it spared neither matrons nor nuns, and spread into adultery and sacrilege. I excited by wine the ardor of my senses, and I was quoted rightly as the hardest drinker in Madaura. I was a Christian, however, and retained in my excesses faith in Christ crucified. After wasting my substance in debauchery, I was beginning to feel the first pangs of poverty, when I saw the most robust of my companions in pleasure rapidly fade away under the attacks of a most terrible malady. His knees could no longer support him; his shaking hands refused to obey him; his darkening eyes closed. His throat gave forth nothing but frightful groans. His mind, more sluggish than his body, slept. For, to punish him for living like a beast, God had changed him into a beast. The loss of my property had already inspired me with salutary reflections; but my friend's example was still more precious; it made such an impression upon my heart that I left the world and returned to the desert. I have enjoyed for twenty years a peace which nothing has disturbed. I follow with my monks the trade of weaver, architect, carpenter, and even scribe, though, to tell the truth, I have little taste for writing, having always preferred action to thought. My days are full of joy and my nights are dreamless, and I think the grace of the Lord is in me, because, in the midst of the most horrible sins, I have always retained hope."

Hearing these words, Paphnutius raised his eyes to heaven, and murmured:

"Lord, thou look'st upon this man soiled by so many crimes, adultery, sacrilege, with gentleness, and thou turnest aside from me who has always observed thy commandments! How obscure is thy justice, O my God! How impenetrable are thy ways!"

Zozimos stretched out his arms:

"Look, venerable father: from the horizon appears what seem to be black files of emigrant ants. Those are our brethren, coming like ourselves to meet Anthony."

When they reached the place of meeting they discovered a magnificent spectacle. The army of hermits extended in an immense semicircle of three rows. The first row was occupied by the ancient inhabitants of the desert, cross in hand, and their beards reaching the ground. The monks ruled by the abbots Ephrem and Serapion, as well as all the Cenobites of the Nile, formed the second row. Behind them stood the ascetics, who had assembled from far distant rocks. Some wore upon their black and withered bodies shapeless rags, others had as clothing rushes bound together with viburnum. Several were naked, but God had covered them with hair as thick as a sheep's fleece. They all held green palms in their hands, they might have been called an emerald rainbow, and they were comparable to the choirs of the elect, or the living walls of the city of God.

The assembly was so perfectly arranged that Paphnutius found without difficulty the monks who were under his rule. He placed himself near them, after taking care to hide his face in his hood, to remain unknown to them and not disturb their religious expectancy. Suddenly a mighty shout arose:

"The Saint," was shouted on all sides. "The Saint, there is the great Saint! there is he, against whom hell has not prevailed, the well-beloved of God! Our father Anthony!"

Then silence reigned, and every forehead was prostrate on the sand.

From the top of a hill in the mighty desert, Anthony advanced, supported by his beloved disciples Macairus and Amathas. He walked slowly, but was upright, and in him could be seen the remnant of superhuman strength. His white beard covered his broad chest, his polished skull reflected rays of light like the forehead of Moses. His eyes were those of an eagle; a childlike smile hovered around his mouth. He rose, to bless his people, though his arms had been wearied by a century of incredible toil, and his voice uttered at last these words of love:

"How beautiful are thy pavilions, Jacob! How amiable are thy tents, Israel!"

Immediately from end to end the living wall resounded like a harmonious roll of thunder with the psalm: "Happy is the man who fears the Lord."

Accompanied by Macairus and Amathas, Anthony traversed the ranks of the old men, the Anchorites and the Cenobites. This man, who had seen heaven and hell, this hermit who, from the top of a rock, had ruled the Christian Church, this saint who had sustained the martyr's faith in the days of supreme trial, this doctor whose eloquence had battered down heresy, spoke tenderly to each of his sons, and wished them familiar adieus, on the eve of his happy death, which God who loved him had at length promised him.

He said to the abbots Ephrem and Serapion:

"You command numerous armies, and you are both illustrious strategists. So will you in heaven be clad in golden armor, and the archangel Michael will give you the title of commanders of his forces."

Seeing the old man Palemon, he kissed him, and said:

"Here is the sweetest and best of my children. His soul gives forth a perfume as fragrant as the flower of the sweet peas he sows each year."

He spoke to the abbot Zozimos thus:

"You have not despaired of divine goodness, therefore the peace of the Lord is in you. The lily of your virtues has flourished upon the filth of your corruption."

His conversation to all of them showed remarkable wisdom.

To the old men he said:

"The apostle saw seated around the throne of God twenty-four old men, clad in white robes, with crowns upon their heads."

To the young men he said:

"Be joyful; leave sorrow to those who are happy in the world."

Thus traversing the front of his filial army, he scattered exhortation broadcast. Paphnutius, seeing him approach, fell upon his knees, torn between fear and hope.

"Father! father!" he cried in anguish, "come to my aid, for I perish. I gave to God the soul of Thaïs. I have dwelt upon the top of a column and in a tomb. My forehead, always on the earth, has become as hard as a camel's knee. But God has departed from me. Bless me, father, and I shall be saved; shake the hyssop, and I shall be washed and shine as the snow."

Anthony did not reply. He cast upon the monks of Antinöe that glance which none could withstand. Letting his eyes rest upon Paul, called the Simple, he considered him long, and then signed to him to approach. As everyone was astounded at the saint addressing a man deprived of his senses, Anthony said:

"God has granted this man more grace than any of you. Lift your eyes, my son Paul, and tell us what you see in the sky."

Paul the Simple raised his eyes; his face shone, and his tongue was loosed.

"I see in the sky a bed adorned with hangings of purple and gold. Around it three virgins vigilantly watch, to see that no soul approaches it, except the elect for whom it is destined."

Believing this bed to be the symbol of his glorification, Paphnutius was already returning thanks to God. But Anthony signed to him to be silent and listen to Paul, who murmured in ecstasy:

"The three virgins speak to me; they say to me: 'A saint is about to leave the earth. Thaïs of Alexandria is about to die. We have set up the bed of her glory, for we are her virtues: Faith, Fear, and Love.'"

Anthony asked:

"Sweet child, what more do you see?" Paul vainly gazed from Zenith to Nadir, from sunset to sunrise, when suddenly his eyes met the priest's of Antinöe. A holy fear paled his face, and his eyes reflected invisible flames.

"I see," he murmured, "three demons who, full of joy, prepare to seize this man. They are like a tower, a woman, and a magician. All three bear their names branded with red hot iron; the first upon the forehead, the second upon the belly, the third upon the breast, and their names are Pride, Luxury, and Doubt.

"I have seen all."

After saying this, Paul, with haggard eyes, and drooping mouth, returned to his state of simplicity.

As the monks of Antinöe looked uneasily at Anthony, the saint pronounced these few words:

"God has made known his righteous judgment. We must adore him and be silent."

He passed, blessing as he went. The sun reached the horizon, enveloping it in glory, and his shadow, enormously increased by the sky's favor, stretched out behind him like an infinite carpet, as a sign of the long souvenir this great saint would leave among men.

Upright, but thunderstruck, Paphnutius saw and heard nothing more. The words that filled his ears were: "Thaïs is about to die!" Such a thought had never come to him. For twenty years he had contemplated a mummy's head, and yet the idea of death extinguishing the eyes of Thaïs desperately astonished him.

"Thaïs is about to die! What a new and horrible sense there is in these words: Thaïs is about to die! Then what need is there for the sun, the flowers, the streams, and all creation? Of what use is the universe?" Suddenly he sprang up. "See her, see her once more!" He began to run. He knew not where he was, but instinct led him with entire certainty; he went straight to the Nile. A swarm of sails covered the waters of the river. He leaped into a bow, manned by Nubians, and there, reclining in the bows, devouring distance with his eyes, he cried in grief and rage:

"Fool that I was not to possess Thaïs while there was yet time! Fool to believe that there was anything in the world but her! Madman! I have thought of God, of my soul's safety, of eternal life, as if all that counted for anything after seeing Thaïs. Why did I not perceive that eternal happiness was in one alone of this woman's kisses, that without her life has no sense, and is only a bad dream? Stupid, you saw her, and yet desired possessions in another world! Coward, you saw her, and feared God! God! Heaven! What is that, and what have they to offer worth the least part of what she

would have given you? O lamentable madman, who sought
divine goodness elsewhere than upon the lips of Thaïs! What
hand was over your eyes? Cursed be the man who blinded
you then! You might have bought for the price of damnation
a moment of her love, and you have not done so. She opened
to you her arms, formed of flesh and the perfume of flowers,
and you did not bury yourself in the unutterable enchantments of her unveiled breast! You listened to the jealous
voice which said to you: 'Abstain.' Dupe, dupe, sad dupe! O
regrets! O remorse! O despair! Not to have the joy of carrying into hell the memory of an ineffaceable hour, and crying
to God: 'Burn my flesh, dry up all the blood in my veins,
shiver my bones into fragments, but you cannot take from
me the recollection which will perfume and refresh me
throughout the centuries! . . . Thaïs is about to die! Ridiculous God, if thou knew'st how I laugh at thy hell! Thaïs is
about to die; she will never be mine, never, never!' "

While the boat drifted with the rapid current, he remained
whole days reclining on his belly repeating:

"Never! Never! Never!"

Then at the idea that she had given herself, and not to him,
that she had scattered over the world waves of love, and that
he had not moistened his lips in them, he stood fiercely up, and
howled with grief. He tore his breast with his nails, and
bit the flesh of his arms. He thought:

"Could I but kill all those she has loved."

The idea of this slaughter filled him with delighted fury.
He meditated devouring Nicias slowly, leisurely, as he looked
deep into his eyes. Then his fury suddenly left him. He wept
and sobbed. He became weak and gentle. An unknown tenderness softened his soul. A desire seized him to throw himself
upon the neck of the companion of his youth and say to him:
"Nicias, I love you, as you loved her. Speak to me of her!
Tell me what she said to you." Without ceasing, the iron of
these words, "Thaïs is about to die," entered his soul.

"Light of day, silver shades of night, stars, heavens, trees with trembling tops, wild beasts, animals, men's anxious souls, do you not understand: 'Thaïs is about to die!' Light, breezes, and perfumes disappear. Forms and thoughts of the universe, efface yourselves! 'Thaïs is about to die!' She was the beauty of the world, and all who approached her were adorned with the reflection of her grace. How amiable were the old man and the sages, who sat near her at the banquet at Alexandria! How harmonious was their conversation! The swarm of laughing smiles hovered on their lips, and pleasure perfumed all their thoughts. And because the breath of Thaïs was upon them, all they said was love, beauty, and truth. Charming impiety lent its grace to their conversation. They easily expressed human splendor. Alas, all that is now only a dream! 'Thaïs is about to die!' Oh, how naturally I shall die of her death! But can you only die, withered embryo, fetus macerated in gall and tears? Miserable abortion, do you think you will taste death, you who never knew life? Provided God exists and damns me! I hope so, I desire it, God, whom I hate, hear me. Cast me into damnation. To compel you to do so I spit in your face. I must find an eternal hell, in which to exhale the eternity of rage which is in me."

.   .   .   .   .   .

At dawn, Albina received the priest of Antinoë on the threshold of the huts.

"You are welcome to our tabernacle of peace, venerable father; for without a doubt you are come to bless the saint you gave us. You know that God in his clemency calls her to him; why should you not know news the angels have borne from desert to desert? It is true that Thaïs approaches her happy end. Her works are ended, and I must tell you in a few words of her conduct while among us. After your departure, as she was shut in the hut marked with your seal, I sent her, with her food, a flute like those the girls of her profession play at feasts. I did this so that she should not become melancholy, nor have less grace and talent before God than she had shown to men's eyes. I acted wisely; for Thaïs every day celebrated on the flute the praises of the Saviour, and the virgins, whom the sounds of the invisible flute attracted, said: 'We hear the nightingale of the celestial groves, the dying swan of Jesus crucified.' Thus was Thaïs accomplishing her penitence, when after sixty days the door you had sealed opened by itself, and the seal of clay broke without being touched by any human hand. At this sign I recognized that the trial you had imposed upon her must cease, and that God pardoned the flute player's sins. From that time she shared the life of my daughters, working and praying with them. She edified them by the modesty of her gestures and words, and she seemed to be the statue of shame among them. Sometimes she was sad; but these clouds passed. When I saw she was attached to God by faith, hope, and love, I did not fear to employ her art and even her beauty for the edification of her sisters. I invited her to represent before us the actions of the brave women and wise virgins of the Scriptures. She imitated Esther, Deborah, Judith, Mary, the sister of Lazarus, and Mary, the mother of Jesus. I know, venerable father, that your austerity is alarmed at the idea of these representations. But you would yourself have been touched if you had seen her, in those pious scenes, burst into real tears and stretch forth her arms like palms to heaven. I have for a long period governed women, and one of my rules is never to counteract their nature. All seeds do not give the same flowers. All souls are not sanctified in the same way. We must also consider that Thaïs gave herself to God when she was still beautiful, and such a sacrifice, if it is not unique, is very rare indeed. This beauty, her robe of nature, has not left her after three months of fever, of which she is dying. As during her illness she ceaselessly asks to see the sky, I have her brought every morning into the courtyard near the well under the ancient fig tree, in whose shade the abbesses of this convent hold their assemblies; you will find her there, venerable father; but hasten, for God calls her, and this evening a shroud will cover the face which God made for the scandal and edification of the world."

Paphnutius followed Albina into the courtyard flooded with the morning light. Along the brick roofs doves formed a string of pearls. Upon a bed, in the shade of the fig tree, Thaïs lay quite white with her arms crossed. Standing by her her side, veiled women recited the prayer of the agony.

"Have pity on me, my God, according to thy great lovingkindness, and wipe out my iniquity according to the multitude of thy mercy!"

He called to her:

"Thaïs."

She lifted her eyelids, and turned in the direction of the voice her white eyeballs. Albina signed to the veiled women to draw back a few steps.

"Thaïs," repeated the monk.

She raised her head; a light whisper came from between her white lips:

"Is it you, father? Do you recollect the water of the fountain and the dates we gathered? That day, father, I was born to love and life."

She ceased to speak, and her head fell back.

Death was upon her, and the sweat of agony crowned her forehead. Breaking the dreadful silence came the plaintive cry of a turtle dove. Then the monk's sobs mingled with the virgins' psalms.

"Wash me from my wickedness and cleanse me from sin. For I know my wickedness and my sin is ever before me."

Suddenly Thaïs rose up in her bed. Her violet eyes opened wide; and with far off looks, and arms outstretched toward the distant hills, she said in a clear and fresh voice:

"There is the rosy dawn of eternal morning."

Her eyes shone; a gentle fervor colored her temples. She lived more sweet and beautiful than ever. Paphnutius, kneeling before her, clasped her in his brown arms.

"Do not die," he cried, in a voice so strange that he did not recognize it himself. "I love you, do not die! Listen, my Thaïs. I have deceived you, and I was but a miserable fool. God, heaven, both are nothing. Nothing is true but life on earth, and carnal love. I love you, do not die. That would be impossible; you are too precious. Come, come with me; I will carry you far in my arms. Come, let us love. Hear me, my beloved, and say: 'I will live. I desire to live.' Thaïs, Thaïs, arise!"

She did not hear him. Her eyes swam in the infinite.

She murmured:

"Heaven is opening. I see angels, prophets, and saints; holy Theodore is among them, his hands full of flowers; he is smiling and calling me. Two seraphim come to me. They approach . . . how beautiful they are! . . . I see God."

She uttered a sigh of pleasure, and her head fell back upon the pillow motionless. Thaïs was dead. Paphnutius, in desperate embrace, devoured her with desire, rage and love.

Albina shouted to him:

"Go away, wretch!"

She gently placed her fingers upon the eyelids of the dead. Paphnutius recoiled, trembling; his eyes were burnt up by flames, and he felt the earth open under his feet.

The virgins intoned the canticle of Zacharias:

"Blessed be the Lord God of Israel."

Suddenly their voices died in their throats. They had seen the priest's face, and fled in fear, crying:

"A vampire! A vampire!"

He had become so hideous that, passing his hand across his face, he could feel his ugliness.

THE END